RATTLED

a mystery

Lisa Harrington

NIMBUS
PUBLISHING

Nimbus Publishing Limited
PO Box 9166
Halifax, NS B3K 5M8
(902) 455-4286 www.nimbus.ca

Printed and bound in Canada

Interior design: Heather Bryan
Front cover: Min Landry
Author photo: Ross Harrington

FSC

Mixed Sources
Product group from well-managed
forests, controlled sources and
recycled wood or fiber

Cert no. SW-COC-003438
www.fsc.org
©1996 Forest Stewardship Council

Library and Archives Canada Cataloguing in Publication

        Harrington, Lisa
        Rattled : a mystery / Lisa Harrington.
        ISBN 978-1-55109-783-1

I. Title.

PS8615.A7473R38 2010   jC813'.6   C2010-903059-1

Canada ▮◆▮   The Canada Council | Le Conseil des Arts   **NOVA SCOTIA**
           for the Arts | du Canada   **Tourism, Culture and Heritage**

We acknowledge the financial support of the Government of Canada through the Book
Publishing Industry Development Program (BPIDP) and the Canada Council, and of the
Province of Nova Scotia through the Department of Tourism, Culture and Heritage for our
publishing activities.

prologue

The blood formed a pool on the floor, surrounded by a kind of circular splatter design. It was like a preschool painting, the ones with the drops of paint squished between a folded piece of paper. There always seemed to be a big glob in the middle. The blood looked just like that.

Flickering through the kitchen, the rotating light from the ambulance made it feel more like a disco than a crime scene. Two officers leaned against the counter talking quietly, taking notes.

The knife had spun, propeller-style, across the floor to rest in front of the fridge. It was now considered evidence.

Outside, pyjama-clad neighbours lined the street, shaking their heads in disbelief. Things like this just didn't happen around here, not in this neighbourhood. At least they didn't before the Swickers moved in.

chapter

1

Five weeks earlier.

It was six days after my fifteenth birthday, and four days into summer vacation. I was bored already. Resting my elbows on the kitchen counter, I watched Mom dice rhubarb as I tried to tune out my sister, Jilly, who was yammering on and on about Robert Pattinson. She'd just come from seeing his movie for the *third* time. I shook my head. Not that I disagree with her—he's totally hot—but she talked about him as though she actually had a chance or something. The fact that she's only a year and a half older than me blew my mind on a daily basis.

"Check the weather, would you, Lydia?" Mom asked.

I flicked on the tiny TV that sat on the top of the fridge, turned to the Weather Network and waited for the local forecast. I used to think it was just *our* family who was obsessed with the weather but now I believe it's all

Maritimers. Probably because our weather changed so quickly, we felt the need to be constantly updated.

"Here we go…Halifax 25, humidex 32," I reported. "But they've got a picture of a sun, a cloud, and raindrops in the little square, so who knows?"

"They just do that to cover their butts," Jilly said.

I looked out the kitchen window to check for myself. The heat was rising up from the street giving off that kind of wavy, watery look. My boredom seemed to be increasing with the temperature.

The entire summer was stretched out before me and I had nothing to do. All my friends were away at cottages, camps, or paddling clubs. It was depressing beyond belief. Even Jilly had a babysitting job. We had no cottage, Mom wasn't the cottagey type. Too much work, she said. Like taking care of two homes.

Okay, so the cottage thing was out, I actually understood that one. And camp? Well, no great loss there, it really wasn't my thing. My idea of roughing it in the wilderness was a Winnebago without a microwave.

I thought I'd come up with the perfect compromise. I'd begged Mom to join the Waeg, a club in the south end of the city. Three pools, tennis, sailing…it was awesome. I told her there were loads of kids that I already knew who went—*loads* being *two*. And after explaining how I could spend the whole day there, be out of her hair, not hanging around the house, I thought she'd be totally sold. I thought wrong.

Should I give it one more try? "Don't suppose you changed your mind about the Waeg?" I asked, still staring out the window.

"You supposed right."

"But Mom, don't you know studies show that teenagers get in trouble fifty percent more often when they're bored?"

"Have you looked in our garage lately? Trust me, I'll make sure you're not bored."

"Mommm," I whined.

"Lydia. I already told you, I'm not spending the summer taxiing you back and forth from downtown."

I spun around and gave Jilly a look. "Well maybe if by some miracle Jilly manages to pass her driving test, *she* could drive. I'd even pay for gas."

"Hey! I've only failed twice, and the last time wasn't my fault! The test lady was wearing navy blue and brown! Together! At the same time! I mean, seriously, how am I supposed to concentrate with that kind of fashion nightmare sitting beside me?!"

I rolled my eyes. "I'll take the bus," I pleaded, turning to face Mom so she could see the desperation in my face.

She looked at me and raised her eyebrows. She knew I was lying.

I had this thing about the bus. There's nothing wrong with it or anything like that, it just made me uncomfortable, especially when I was by myself. It felt like people were staring at me. Whenever I got on or off, I could *feel* their eyes following me. They probably weren't. I knew people had better things to do than observe my every move, but my neck would still break out in a nervous rash every time. That sounds paranoid, and I'm so not. Well…maybe just a bit, but only on the bus.

"There's this new thing," Jilly said. "Maybe you've heard of it? It's called a *job*?"

Easy for her to say, sitting there all smug. She'd landed the most coveted summer job in the neighbourhood—babysitting for the Darcys. They paid a bijillion dollars an hour, had the best snacks, and their kids were angels. Jilly could look forward to many hours of texting, painting her nails, and lying in the sun—three of her greatest talents.

Mom wiped her hands on the dishtowel. "We really should look into that, Lydia. There must be something…maybe Dad could use you at the office…"

My shoulders slumped. I wasn't *that* bored. I turned back to the window, willing something to happen. When I was a kid I thought I possessed some kind of telekinetic power— that I could make something happen with my mind if I concentrated hard enough. Okay…I still sort of think it. Like the other night in the car, I was looking at a street light, and *poof*, it burned out. I figure that's got to be *some* kind of power. I mean, what else could it be?

My ears perked up at the sound of squeaking brakes.

"Check it out," I said. *Maybe I do possess some powers after all.*

A beat-up Volkswagen camper van pulled up to the curb in front of the house directly across the street. It was bright orange speckled with a bunch of rust patches.

Apparently Jilly and Mom hadn't heard me. Jilly was trying to convince Mom that in a few years, the age difference between her and Robert wouldn't mean a thing.

"I think someone finally rented the Henleys' house," I said loudly, over my shoulder.

Mom and Jilly rushed over to join me at the window.

"It's about time," Mom said. "That sign's been up for months."

"Well, I hope they have some boys." Jilly smoothed her hair with her hands.

"Would you give it a rest, Jilly? There's more to life, you know." She was too annoying for words.

"I don't know what your problem is, Lid, it's not like you've never had a *thing* for a boy, so why don't *you* give it a rest?"

I sucked in my breath. I knew what she was referring to, that momentary lapse in judgment last fall. In my defense, it only lasted four days. My best friend William asked my other best friend Vicki "out." On a real date! Talk about messing up the trio. I couldn't believe it! If he wanted a girlfriend, why wouldn't he have just picked me? I mean, I probably would have said no, but still, wasn't I the obvious choice? I'd known him for like *ever*. It really bugged me. I sulked for days, *four* days. That's how long it took me to realize they had basically turned bipolar, sickeningly lovey-dovey one minute, paranoid and depressed the next. Not to mention when they were apart, all they did was text each other. It was nauseating. Who needs that?

Jilly whispered, "*Lid and William sitting in a tree…*" into my ear.

I gave her a dirty look and elbowed her in the ribs. I hated when she called me Lid.

"Knock it off, you two," Mom said.

The three of us pressed our faces closer to the window and waited for the van door to slide open.

"Ouch!" I yelled. Jilly had my arm in a death grip and was digging her fingernails into my flesh.

"Look!" She was practically jumping up and down.

I rubbed my arm and followed her gaze to see what the big deal was. Then I saw it. *Him. Him* was beautiful. I hated to admit it, but I think my mouth actually fell open.

"He's stretching!" Jilly shrieked, right into my ear.

I moved out of her reach before she did permanent damage. I continued to watch the scene outside unfold. Dragging my eyes from the boy, I noticed a girl. She was blonde and beautiful, just like the boy. She looked about my age. Hmmm…the boy was probably older? Maybe about Jilly's age? Was there no justice?

Then there was the mother. She wasn't blonde *or* beautiful. The word *sharp* popped into my head, and not the good kind. Tall, thin, pale, all pointy angles and edges, like a villain straight out of a Disney movie. A black cat appeared and circled the mother's legs. I smiled, thinking how appropriate that somehow seemed.

"What should we do?" Jilly asked, wringing her hands.

"Well, you could go over, say hi, introduce yourself," Mom suggested.

"Oh yes! That's *exactly* what we should do." Jilly turned and grabbed me by the shoulders. I cringed, bracing for the pain. "Go fix yourself up and we'll go over together."

I squirmed out of her grasp. "It's okay, I think I'm good to go."

She gave me a quick once over and shrugged her shoulders. "Suit yourself."

I watched her bend at the waist, swing her head full of blonde hair back and forth a couple times, then straighten up. It was like watching a shampoo commercial. I sighed as she pulled out a tube of lip gloss, whipping the wand around with unimaginable precision and speed. She didn't even use a mirror. I was still shaking my head when we left the house.

The new neighbours were milling around the van, lifting out assorted boxes and suitcases, when we arrived in their driveway. The boy put down the box he was holding and smiled when he saw us. I really wished I had fixed my hair and put on some lip gloss.

No one seemed to want to speak first, so I took the plunge. "Hi."

"Welcome to the neighbourhood," Jilly gushed.

"I'm Lydia," I said.

"And I'm Jilly."

The girl came and stood by the boy. The mother remained on the other side of the van, talking on her cellphone.

"I'm Sam," the boy said. "This is my sister, Megan, and that's," he gestured with his head, "our mom."

"Hi." The girl smiled shyly and gave a tiny wave.

I fiddled with my watch strap, trying to come up with something intelligent to say. "So...where you guys coming from?"

The mother snapped her cellphone shut and joined our circle.

"Ottawa," she answered for them. "We've just come from Ottawa."

"Mom, this is Lydia and Jilly. They live across the street," Sam said.

"Hmmm, yes, I can see that."

"My friend Daisy moved to Ottawa three years ago," I said. "We drive up for Easter every year. Where'd you live in Ottawa?"

Again it was the mother who answered. "A small place. I'm sure you've never heard of it."

"Did it have a mall?" Jilly piped up.

The mother seemed confused by the question. "Yes..."

"Then chances are we were probably there. See, I'm a bit

of a shopaholic," Jilly said, talking out of the corner of her mouth. "I'm sure there isn't a mall in Ottawa I haven't been to."

"That's nice," the mother said, then turned to the kids. "Megan. Take that cooler inside and put the things in the fridge." Her cellphone rang and she stepped away to answer it.

Jilly threw me a "would ya get a load of her" look.

"Well, it was nice to meet you," Megan said politely. She seemed a bit embarrassed.

"Yeah, you too. Things can get kind of boring around here in the summer."

Megan smiled another shy smile and bent over to pick up the cooler.

"Now it's *so* not boring," Jilly added, making her lips kind of pouty and giving Sam her best *Next Top Model* look.

I rolled my eyes. She was at it already.

Sam swiftly intercepted the cooler from Megan. "I'll take that for you, Meg. It's heavy." He turned to us. "So…maybe we'll see you around."

"Definitely," Jilly and I answered in unison, both nodding like a couple of Bobblehead dolls, *idiot* Bobblehead dolls.

The mother returned. "Yes, well, we're going to be busy for quite a while." She looked at me and Jilly like we were something she'd scraped off the bottom of her shoe. "There's a lot to be done. Megan, get Peter and take him inside."

Megan quickly scooped up the cat.

Before Jilly or I could even say bye, the mother corralled Sam and Megan and herded them up the driveway.

Jilly and I just stood there looking after them, and then at each other.

"Well *that* was kind of weird," I said.

"No kidding. Who names a cat Peter?"

I raised my eyebrows. "I'm talking about—"

"Duh," she interrupted, giving me a shove. "The mother…I know. She seriously needs a personality transplant or something."

"She never *did* tell us where they lived in Ottawa. Did you notice that?"

"Yeah well, let's forget her and focus on *other* things."

"Oh, I know what *you're* focusing on."

"And by the way, I call first dibs, you know, on Sam," she clarified.

"What? What about Clark?"

"Clark?!" she exclaimed. "He's like *so* last week!"

I stopped and stared at her. I could have sworn Clark had been standing in our kitchen…well…just the week before… so I guess she was right.

"It's a lot of work finding your soulmate," she continued. "Sam might be the one, you know."

What could I say? "Fine," I muttered under my breath. *Curse* the law of first dibs.

We walked across the street. Jilly started humming. I knew she was lost in her own world, probably picturing how Sam would look in a tux taking her to the prom. *I* was thinking about the mother. Besides the obvious, there was just something I couldn't put my finger on.

And then I felt it, the hairs prickled on the back of my neck. I glanced sideways at Jilly—still humming. I didn't have to turn around to know the mother was watching us. It reminded me of being on the bus. The only difference...I knew I wasn't being paranoid this time.

chapter

2

"What do you mean you don't know their last name?" Mom asked. She had been watching us from the kitchen window and wanted a full report.

"Mom, we don't talk about stuff like that," Jilly said.

"What's that supposed to mean? When you meet new people, don't you ask them their names?"

"Well, we got their *first* names. The kids are Megan and Sam," I said.

"They're from Ottawa," Jilly added.

"Oh, for the love of God, pass me my coffee cake pan," Mom demanded, opening cupboards and slamming down baking ingredients.

"Mom, settle down. You're acting like we've disgraced the family name or something," I said.

"Plus, the mother's a real piece of work. *Craaan-key*," Jilly said. "She doesn't strike me as the coffee cake type. Did you see how skinny she was, Lid? She kind of reminds me of Mrs.

Wilson, remember? We used to say she lived on her church communion wafer."

I laughed. I did remember Mrs. Wilson. Grade six French. She was at least a hundred years old, and all of eighty pounds. I always felt nervous that she was going to drop dead in the middle of class. Our new neighbour could totally be her daughter. Well, maybe her granddaughter.

"Jilly's right, Mom, it might be a waste of chocolate chips." I grabbed a handful out of the bag.

"Well, there *is* Sam and Megan…" Jilly passed Mom the eggs.

"Yeah, I guess."

Jilly and I sat at the table, flipping through a pile of flyers as Mom whipped up her famous coffee cake. Soon the kitchen was filled with the smell of chocolate and cinnamon. In no time at all, the oven timer went off.

"I'm going to change and let that cool a bit," Mom informed us. "Then I'm going to take it over and welcome them to the neighbourhood." She sounded a little angry, like her having to bake a cake at the drop of a hat was somehow *our* fault.

"What's her problem?" Jilly asked.

"Didn't you hear the 'if you want something done right, you better do it yourself' tone in her voice?"

"Ohhh," she nodded. "Gotcha."

"You don't think we have to go with her, do you?"

Jilly pressed her lips together and squished them around, like she was reactivating her lip gloss. "I'll go. I wouldn't mind seeing Sam again."

That helped me decide. "Yeah, I guess I'll go too."

Mom reappeared, hair all neat, clothes free of flour. "Are you coming with me?"

"Yup," we answered.

Once again we trekked across the street. The coffee cake led the parade.

Mom rang the bell. We waited.

The door opened. It was the scary mother.

"Welcome to the neighbourhood," Mom said, holding out the cake.

The scary mother put her hand to her throat. "Oh my, I don't know what to say. How very lovely. Won't you come in?"

Jilly and I shot each other a look and followed Mom into the house.

"Sam! Megan!" the scary mother called. "Those *lovely* girls from across the street are here."

I felt like I was in a parallel universe or something.

"I'm Justine, Justine Tanner," Mom said.

"I'm Bernadette Swicker." She reached out and took the cake. Scary mother now had a name.

Sam and Megan arrived slightly out of breath. "Sorry, we were trying to get the TV working, but I don't think the cable's been hooked up yet," Sam said.

I nodded sympathetically, hoping he would sense how much I shared his frustration. I happened to catch a glimpse of Jilly doing the exact same thing. I wanted to kick her.

"Shall I make some tea, Justine? And cut into this beautiful cake?" Mrs. Swicker asked.

"No, no, we're not going to impose, you're trying to get settled in. I hope it turned out though, it was a bit of a rush job. We didn't know you were coming."

"Oh, I don't eat sweets, but I'm sure it's perfect." Mrs. Swicker handed the cake to Megan.

I felt Jilly nudge me.

"Oh." Mom seemed at a loss for words.

"Well, thank you for making us feel so welcome," Mrs. Swicker smiled.

I noticed her smile didn't quite reach her eyes.

"My pleasure. It's nice to have some new neighbours on the street." Mom ushered us towards the door.

Jilly and I speed-walked home and impatiently waited for Mom. We practically pulled her in the door and both started talking at once.

"Stop!" Mom put up her hands. "I can't understand a word, but I'll start off by saying, I thought Mrs. Swicker seemed perfectly fine."

"But Mom, she's not. And what about the not eating sweets thing?" Jilly sputtered.

"Well that doesn't make her a bad person. I thought she was quite friendly," Mom said.

"Mom! She wasn't like that this morning. She was all *snippy*-like."

"Lid's right, Mom, she was looking down her nose at us the whole time."

"Let me tell you, she sure wasn't all rainbows and puppy dogs, like you just saw," I said.

Mom sighed one of those giant mother-like sighs. "Girls, did it ever occur to you that she may have been tired, maybe she'd been driving for hours, *maybe* you didn't catch her at her best moment?"

A couple seconds of silence ticked by.

"I guess," Jilly mumbled.

Mom turned to me for my response. She was trying to stare me down. "Lydia?"

"Anything's possible." I knew it was just easier to give her the answer she wanted.

"Thank you both for being so open-minded," Mom said. "We wouldn't want to jump to any wrong conclusions."

She might as well have added, "would we, Lydia?" I knew that was what she was thinking.

I tilted my head, smiled sweetly, and took off to my room. With the door safely closed, I went to the window, opened it wide to let in some breeze, and stared across the street. I watched Megan walk to the van, lift out a suitcase, and head up the driveway. Sam met her halfway, took the case from her, and returned to the house.

I must have watched Megan and Sam make a half a dozen trips to that van while I stood there chewing on a hangnail, safely hidden behind a curtain panel. They were working so hard, I almost thought that maybe I should go over and offer to help.

"Don't dilly-dally!" Mrs. Swicker hollered from the front step. "Sam, just get your violin. Megan can finish up. You should be practising."

I saw Sam grab his violin case and go back inside.

A few minutes later, the faint sound of violin drifted in through my open window. It was beautiful. I could almost swear it was coming from a CD.

I got a little overzealous in my hangnail chewing and had to grab a Kleenex to wrap up my bleeding finger. I didn't want to leave the window to get a Band-Aid, I was too worried I might miss something. Good thing. It was Mrs. Swicker. She was carrying a box and heading towards their green bin against the side of the house.

My room was on the second floor, so I had a pretty good view of their whole yard. Mrs. Swicker set the box down in front of the green bin, glanced at our house, and checked behind her over one shoulder, then the other. Seemingly satisfied no one was watching, she bent down and lifted something out of the box.

I gasped. That was Mom's blue cake plate. That was Mom's cake!

Mrs. Swicker opened the lid and slid the cake in.

I don't know if I was more stunned or offended. I wanted to scream across the street, "Hey, you ungrateful troll!" But then what? I wanted to call Mom and Jilly to the window, but I knew it was too late, they'd already missed it. I could *tell* them what happened. Jilly might believe me. Mom would probably say something like I just *thought* I saw the cake, it could have been *anything*. Not to mention, she would consider all this to fall under the heading of jumping to conclusions. It was a lose-lose situation, so I did nothing.

I continued to stare across the street for a long time after the action died down. I got the distinct feeling this wasn't going to be the last time I would do this—stare across the street at the Swickers'.

chapter

3

It had been a few days, and I was still wondering if I should
have told anyone about what I saw in the driveway, about
the dumping of the cake. *Might be kind of interesting when
Mrs. Swicker decides to return the plate, though. I'll definitely
have to make sure I'm home for that one.*

More days passed, and still no sign of the cake plate. I can't
explain it, but for some reason I was feeling very territorial
about Mom's plate. It was turning into an obsession.

In the meantime, I managed to spend a bit of time with
Sam and Megan. I was curious about them, wanted to get to
know them. It was all small talk at first, mostly just speaking
to each other from across the street. Like, "Is it hot enough
for ya?" "Are you all unpacked?" "Is your cable working yet?"
That kind of thing.

There was a basketball hoop mounted over their garage
door, so one day I brought them over an extra basketball we
had in our shed. Sam was grateful, and spent a lot of time

shooting hoops. Sometimes I'd play with him, sometimes I'd lean against the stone wall with Megan, yak, and just watch. Yeah…the watching was good.

The bonus was it made Jilly mental. She wasn't so smug about her great job now. She was missing all these chances to be around Sam. I *did* notice she was suddenly a health nut—taking the Darcy kids for walks, biking, all right in front of our house.

"Uh…Jilly? You should take them biking over on Lynwood, it's perfectly flat," I suggested one afternoon.

"No. This is fine," she replied, twisting a piece of hair around her finger, eyes glued to Sam.

I raised my eyebrows and stared down the massively steep hill that was our street.

The Darcy kids were staring down it too, worried looks on their faces.

• • •

I discovered Sam and Megan both loved to read. So did I. We talked about books we liked and didn't like, books made into movies, and books that *should* be made into movies. I had the exact same opinions as Sam—go figure. It was obvious they travelled a lot, just from things they said. I found out they were originally from San Diego. But they never mentioned their father, and I didn't feel right asking.

Even as I was learning all these little tidbits about them, the cake plate was never far from my mind. So many times

I wanted to say, "So…how was the coffee cake?" I didn't know if they knew the fate of the cake. They must have wondered what happened to it, though. Either way, it would be awkward. And anyhow, Mrs. Swicker always seemed to be around or would appear whenever we struck up a conversation that lasted more than five minutes. I've never seen anyone so dedicated to weeding the garden. If I didn't know better, I'd say she planted new weeds in the dead of night just so she could take them out the next day while she eavesdropped. I knew she was listening to every word we said.

Loads of times, I invited Sam and Megan to hang out at my place. Mrs. Swicker always said no, they had stuff to do. It made me nuts.

Between this mysterious *stuff*, and the cake plate, it was like I couldn't think of anything else. My mind wouldn't shut off at night. Every morning it felt like I'd slept for maybe two minutes and this morning was no different.

I finished making my bed and went down to the kitchen.

"Dad! You're back."

"Hi, Pumpkin. Got in late last night." He stood at the stove stirring a frying pan full of eggs. "Want some breakfast?"

"Did you put Tabasco in there?"

"Of course!"

"Uh…no thanks." You'd think after fifteen years, he'd catch on that he's the only one who likes a half a bottle of hot sauce in scrambled eggs. "So how was your conference?"

"Great! Nothing says fun like a convention of dermatologists," he chuckled.

I shook my head as he stood there in his Heineken T-shirt, boxers, and slippers with sport socks pulled up to his knees.

"I hear we got some new neighbours," he said.

"Yup."

"According to your mother, the young man's quite a 'hottie.'"

"Ewww, Dad!"

"What? Am I not hip to your jive?"

"Dad! Stop!" It was like fingernails down a chalkboard.

Dad rolled his eyes. "So what do we know about these people?"

"Not a lot. The mother's kind of…well…too hard to describe. The parents must be divorced or something. The kids are nice. They're kind of quiet, though. But anytime we get talking or I ask them a question, *poof*, there's Mrs. Swicker, sticking her nose in."

"Maybe she's just the overprotective type."

I didn't comment.

"You'll just have to win over this Mrs. Swicker. You know, kill her with kindness."

"I dunno…"

"Where's your sister? I haven't seen her this morning."

"She slept over at Ellen's. She was going to the Darcys' from there."

"Oh?"

"It's okay. Phase One of her grounding ended yesterday."

Dad nodded but didn't look very pleased.

A few weeks before, Jilly had gone to an end of exams bash. It had been the party all future parties would be compared to. The number of groundings that were handed out the morning after broke a new neighbourhood record. Vicki, William, and I actually managed to crash the party for all of twelve minutes. That was until some of Jilly's friends spotted us. We weren't officially in high school yet, so there was no way we were allowed to stay. The party thrower and quarterback of the West football team immediately escorted us to the door.

Then later that night, Vicki's dad had been out walking the dog and found Jilly, arms wrapped around the stop sign, puking her guts out. He brought her home. Man, I would have donated a kidney to have been awake for that one—you can't put a price on entertainment like that.

"What's Phase Two again?" Dad asked.

"Hour off the curfew. Then comes probation, then maintenance." If I didn't know better, I'd think Mom consulted Weight Watchers when she developed her punishment pyramid. Come to think of it, she *is* a lifetime member.

"Must keep an eye on that girl," Dad said to himself, then looked at me. "So…speaking of summer jobs…"

I narrowed my eyes. "We weren't."

"Mom said you're bored, might be looking for work."

"Ummm."

"I'll need someone when Kelley goes on vacation. It would just be answering phones, taking appointments, that kind of thing."

I tugged on my lower lip, trying to think of a response. I had kind of always hoped when I landed a summer job it would be a bit more glamorous, not working in my dad's dermatology clinic where the only boys I'd meet would, let's face it, have complexion issues.

"I thought I might check up at Northcliff Tennis Club." I'd always thought that would be sort of a glam place to work.

"Well, Pumpkin…you don't play tennis," he said gently.

"There's always Kearney Lake. They might need lifeguards." Another awesomely glam job.

"I think you have to have lifeguard training," he pointed out.

"Right," I nodded. I was running out of glamorous job options. "Okay, Dad. Guess I'm your girl."

He beamed. "Great! You can make your own schedule, a couple mornings, maybe an afternoon, still lots of time to do your own thing."

That wouldn't be so bad. And I *was* going to be needing a whole new wardrobe for starting high school. I should have been grateful. "Thanks, Dad. I'm psyched."

chapter

I kept Dad company while he ate his eggs. I tried not to laugh when he gasped for water on the last bite.

"Too much salt," he puffed, slamming his empty glass down on the counter. He'd burst into flames before he'd admit he made the eggs too hot.

"Sure, Dad," I smirked. "Where's Mom?"

He flipped open the dishwasher. "She forgot it was Nana Mary's birthday, so she's out in the driveway spray-painting some old planters. She's going to throw in some plants from the garden, pass them off as new. Is it any wonder I love that woman?"

I smiled. Dad totally cracked me up.

I went outside to check on Mom's progress. "Those look great!"

"Thanks. Let's face it, she's ninety-six, she probably won't even be able to see them clearly."

I heard the smack of the basketball hitting the pavement

and looked up. Sam and Megan were playing one-on-one. I waved and walked over.

"Hey. Who's winning?"

"Me, for once," Megan said, pushing the hair out of her eyes.

"I'm letting her," Sam whispered.

"Sam." Mrs. Swicker magically appeared, as usual. "I told you, I'm not too crazy about you playing so much basketball. Your hands, your fingers. Maybe you should just return the ball to Lydia."

"Good morning, Bernadette!" Mom yelled from across the street.

Mrs. Swicker jumped, startled. "Oh, hello, Justine." She gave a weak wave.

Mom dusted off her hands and joined us in the driveway. "All settled in now?"

"Yes, thank you," Mrs. Swicker answered stiffly.

I sensed there was some kind of shift, something had changed. A tiny voice in my head urged me to invite Sam and Megan over, *again*. I knew I should be taking advantage of the fact that Jilly was babysitting all the time. I could have Sam all to myself. Oh, and Megan too. I stepped around Mrs. Swicker. "You guys want to come over and play some Ping-Pong?"

"Can we, Mom?" Sam asked.

Mrs. Swicker's eyes darted around the circle of people awaiting her answer. "Fine. Just for a while."

Miracle of miracles. You could have knocked me over with a feather. It took me a second to put it all together, but the shift was that Mom was there. I think Mrs. Swicker didn't want to say no in front of her.

"Come on." I didn't want to give Mrs. Swicker a chance to change her mind.

We hurried across the street and downstairs to the rec room.

I picked up the paddles. "Do you know how to play?"

"No. We'll learn as we go," Sam said.

"Okay," I said. "How about we do a rotation?"

Sam and I started, hitting the ball back and forth to each other as I gave him some instructions and a few pointers.

"So…how long have you played the violin?" I asked. If trashy teenage TV dramas have taught me anything, it's that boys are impressed if you show interest in things *they're* interested in.

His face lit up. "For as long as I can remember. Someday I'd love to play with a real orchestra, maybe even write music."

"Wow. My big goal is to get through all five seasons of *Lost* before the end of the summer."

He laughed.

"Do you play anything, Megan?"

"She's a fantastic piano player," Sam said proudly. He went on to explain how there had been a piano at one of the houses they'd rented, and Megan had taught herself to play.

"That's amazing. I think I must be tone deaf or something. No musical talent whatsoever," I said as I rubbed the back of my head. I'd banged it on the corner of the table picking up the ball for the umpteenth time. Sam wasn't very good at Ping-Pong.

We switched partners, Sam and Megan played. I was ball girl. I was very busy.

After a while they got into a bit of a groove. As they volleyed back and forth, it gave me the chance to openly check Sam out. I wondered if he watched *Gossip Girl*—the way his bangs were super long in the front and they fell across his eyes, he really had a Chace Crawford thing going on. There was no doubt about it, he was going to be the cutest guy at school. I felt a little burst of joy inside knowing I would already have the inside track—I'd be the envy of every girl at the West.

"Later we should walk over to the school. You might want to check it out," I suggested. "What grade are you guys going into anyway?"

"Meg ten, me twelve," Sam said.

"So, Megan, we might be in some of the same classes. Sam, you could end up in some of Jilly's." It made my throat hurt to finish the sentence.

That's when Sam broke the news. They were home-schooled.

I couldn't think of anything to say. I felt totally deflated. Apparently home-schooling was the way to go because they moved so much. They moved so much because Mrs. Swicker was a photographer and she liked to change locations constantly.

I remained quiet for a long time, trying to get my head around this new development. It was a real bummer. "I wish you weren't. Home-schooled, that is."

"Oh, it's not so bad," Sam said cheerfully, serving and hitting Megan's shoulder with the ball.

"Really?" I sounded doubtful. "Don't you ever wish you could go to regular school?"

Sam frowned. "Never really thought about it. I kind of like that we only have lessons for maybe three hours a day."

"I guess…" I still wasn't too happy about it all.

"Wanna switch?" Megan asked. "I'm really bad at this."

My stomach growled. I suggested we go up to the kitchen and get a snack instead.

As I got down three glasses, I saw a head bounce by the window, then heard the door open.

"Morning, Tanner family!"

Crap! "Hi, Vivian!" I called.

"Is Jilly around?" Vivian asked, bursting onto the scene.

"No. She won't be back until five."

"Oh. I'm just dropping off this book she wanted to borrow." She was looking past me, at Sam and Megan.

"You must have misunderstood her," I said. "Jilly doesn't read."

She smirked and wagged her finger at me. "I don't care *what* Jilly says about you, I think you're just *precious*." She practically shoved me aside. "You must be the new neighbours."

Vivian was Jilly's best friend. There was no way she didn't know Jilly babysat until five—this was an obvious fishing expedition. Vivian's eyes zeroed in on Sam. It was almost comical. I felt like throwing my body in front of him like a shield.

"Vivian Green, this is Sam and Megan Swicker," I said, begrudgingly.

Vivian glanced briefly at Megan and smiled, then turned the full force of her powers on Sam. "En-chanté…" She held out her hand.

I sighed with relief when Sam gave her an odd look, reached out, and awkwardly shook her finger. "Uh…nice to meet you."

"It's going to be so lovely to have some fresh faces in school this year," she cooed. "I just live one street over, so if…"

"Home-schooled!" I shouted.

"Oh." Her face fell.

"Okay then." I put my hand on her shoulder and steered her towards the door. "I'll tell Jilly you stopped by."

"She seemed nice," Sam said, when I rejoined them in the kitchen.

"Well, she's not. It'd be in your best interest to avoid her at all costs."

"She can't be *that* bad," Sam said.

"Listen. Like six years ago or something, she was a runner up on *America's Funniest Home Videos*. She thinks she's a friggin' celebrity and she treats everyone like peasants. She's just the *worst*."

"What'd she do on the video?"

"It was something about her lunatic cat destroying the Christmas tree. God, she was only in it for a nanosecond, but for some reason she thinks she's a star. Plus, I didn't think Canadians were even allowed to enter!" I added, slamming the fridge door.

Sam and Megan both laughed. They drank their juice but said no thanks to a snack.

I made myself a peanut butter and jelly fold-over, and we headed back for more ping-pong.

We hadn't been downstairs for more than two minutes when I heard the doorbell. I strained my ear. Mom or Dad must have answered.

"Sam. Megan. Your mom's here!" Mom called.

"Oh…We didn't get to finish," I complained.

Following them up the stairs, I checked my watch. Almost noon. Mrs. Swicker had let them out of her sight for all of forty-five minutes.

Sam and Megan thanked me and said goodbye, so did Mrs. Swicker. I could tell it caused her great pain, but Mom and Dad were standing right there. I know she felt she had to.

I went into the kitchen to wash some grape jelly off my shirt.

Damn! I missed it. The blue cake plate was on the counter.

chapter

5

So I thought I'd be neighbourly, share my great idea. The van was in the driveway, I knew they were home. I ran a brush through my hair, dabbed on a little lip gloss, did that sideways thing in the mirror smoothing out my T-shirt and shorts, and headed across the street.

Standing on their front step, I listened to the doorbell echo through the house. I heard footsteps and then Mrs. Swicker opened the door. Her face fell when she realized it was me. I'm not making that up, she looked positively crestfallen and she didn't bother to hide it.

"Yes?" she sighed.

"Hi," I said brightly. "Megan and Sam home?"

"No."

Her answer caught me off guard. "No?"

She put her hand on her hip and leaned toward me. "I think I would know whether or not my kids were home."

As I pulled back I thought I caught a whiff of something

on her breath—alcohol? "Yeah, ummm, of course," I stuttered. "Just tell them…" The door closed in my face. "That I was looking for them…" My voice trailed off.

I marched down their front steps shaking my head. I must have imagined the smell. It wasn't even ten o'clock. She definitely OD'd on her nasty pills, though. I couldn't imagine my mom treating any of my friends like that, even the ones she's not too crazy about. Why did Mrs. Swicker have it in for me? Dad says I'm so sweet I give him cavities.

Back home and still a little ticked, I threw two pieces of bread in the toaster and slammed down the lever. I stared out the kitchen window at their house, wishing I had x-ray vision so I could see what in the world was going on behind those walls.

"What the…?"

There was Megan, walking across her driveway, carrying some stuff to the van. Okay, was this some mass conspiracy? Up until now I'd thought it was just their bizzarro mother.

I ran out the front door. "Megan!" I shouted.

She looked up and waved. "Hey!"

I crossed the street to meet her. "I was just at your house. Your mom said you weren't home." I stared at her intently, looking for telltale signs of deception.

"You were?" She looked genuinely surprised. "I heard the bell. Mom said it was some kid collecting bottles for a bottle drive."

We both stood there, looking at each other, frowning in deep concentration.

"I can't imagine why she'd tell you that," Megan continued, scrunching up her nose.

"Beats me," I shrugged.

"Maybe she misunderstood. What did you say?"

"Not a lot. She pretty much slammed the door in my face."

"Oh…sorry," she said, apologetically.

"I mean, no offense, but I just don't get it. Does she always act that way with your friends, or just with me?"

Megan took her time answering. "Well, since we move so much, we don't get the chance to make a lot of friends."

"Oh." I sort of felt bad.

"She's just not what you'd call a people person, I guess. So, like, don't let it bother you." She kept sneaking peeks over my shoulder towards her house, like she was watching for something or someone.

I couldn't help it. I turned my head to follow her line of vision. The curtain moved in the window.

"Oh, okay then," I said slowly.

"So what did you want when you came over?"

I got the feeling she was trying to change the subject. "Right. I thought we could plan a day down at the waterfront. I could show you and Sam all the touristy things. You know, 'all the things Halifax has to offer'?"

"Umm…maybe." She slid her ring up and down her finger.

"I don't know if Mom…"

I sighed heavily. "Let me guess, you don't think your mom will let you."

"No, no, she might…" Megan said, shaking her head. "It's just like she has this thing about letting us do stuff with people she doesn't know, that's all, no big deal."

"But she *knows* me," I pointed out.

"Really, like I said, she's just not a people person." Megan was beginning to look uncomfortable.

There was an awkward pause. I cleared my throat. "Okay, then. I should probably…"

"Yeah, I gotta get back inside." She pulled the van door closed, and hurried up the driveway.

I stood and watched her. There was something weird about the whole thing. *Not a people person, that's the understatement of the year. I think she's just a big control freak with a little bit of crazy thrown in.*

I stuck out my bottom lip. Megan didn't seem a bit excited over my great idea. If it were me, I'd be jumping at the chance to get away from Mrs. Swicker, even for a day.

Maybe Sam would be a little more receptive to my great idea. As soon as I saw him, I'd corner him and ask. It'd never actually been just him and me. I couldn't wait to wow him with my witty repartee.

The rest of the morning I spent basically staking out their house. *Now who's crazy?* So Mom wouldn't get suspicious as to why I was lurking around the kitchen, I mixed up a batch of chocolate chip cookies. I could see the Swickers' front and garage doors perfectly out our kitchen window. Pulling the last tray of cookies out of the oven, I finally detected movement. It was as I'd hoped—Sam. He was crushing up a pile of cardboard boxes in the driveway. I grabbed two cookies off the cooling rack, wrapped them in paper towel, and rushed out to the street.

"Sam! Hey!"

"Hey, what's up?" he asked, dumping the cardboard on the grass.

He had on a baby blue golf shirt. It was the exact colour of his eyes. He stood there waiting for me to speak. There was a fluttery feeling in my chest. I realized I'd forgotten what I wanted to ask him.

"Right, right," I mumbled under my breath. "So...I was talking to Megan a while ago." I tried to sound casual.

"Yeah, she told me."

"She did? Did she tell you what we talked about?"

"Uh huh."

"Did she tell you what your mom did? About me coming to the door?"

"Yeah."

I found it odd he had no further comment. "Oh." *So much for my witty repartee.* "She told you about my great idea? About going downtown and spending the day on the waterfront? There's loads of stuff to do and see. The museum, the *Bluenose*, great shops, places to eat." I realized I was gushing, that I was trying too hard to sell it. "You could help me plan the itinerary, over cookies," I added, holding out the paper towel. I took a step forward, more of a *mis*-step really, forgetting I was standing on the curb. I lost my balance, my dignity, and my chocolate chip cookies.

I jumped up quickly. Maybe by some miracle he hadn't noticed. There was always the hope he suffered from temporary blindness. "I'm okay!" I announced loudly, then winced in pain.

Sam rushed to my side. "Here, just sit down for a second." Holding my elbow, he guided me down onto the grass.

Even though this wasn't quite how I'd pictured it playing out, it wasn't so bad. There was that fluttery feeling again and I leaned on him a little extra. "I'm fine, really, it's nothing." I still felt like a total loser. Like how much of a spaz must I be to fall off the curb? Off the curb! The fact that he smelled really good somehow made the whole thing a bit more bearable.

He sat down beside me on the grass while I rubbed and rotated my ankle.

"So you want us to go on some massive adventure, huh?"

I nodded. "Yeah, it would be totally awesome, I know you'd love it."

"Well…I'm not sure if Mom…"

"Argh! That's what Megan said. Does your mother really hate me that much?"

He looked surprised, fake surprised. "No, she thinks you're great." He would never have to worry about winning an Oscar.

I almost laughed in his face. It was a combination of what he said and the unconvincing way he said it. But I didn't. It might embarrass him, wouldn't want to do that.

"If you say so," I shrugged.

"Yeah, I think she's still tired from the move. She's really not a people person."

You don't say.

"It's almost like…" He scrunched up his nose just like Megan.

"Let me guess," I interrupted. "Like she has a *thing* about letting you do stuff with people she doesn't know."

He frowned. "Yeah."

"Megan told me the same thing," I explained. *The exact same thing, almost like they rehearsed it.*

"Well…that's how it is."

"Guess I'll just go out of my way to get to know her, so she'll feel comfortable around me." I didn't really mean it. I just wanted to see what he'd say.

"You don't have to do anything like that. I told you, she thinks you're great," he said, without looking me in the eye.

"No really, I can be *ultra* charming when I want to be." I batted my eyelashes for special effect.

He forced a smile. "It just takes her a while to warm up to people."

"*Riiiight*." My eyebrows were raised so high my face hurt.

"Look, I'll let you know what I can arrange for that trip downtown. I'll talk to Mom, okay?" He stood and reached out his hand to help me up. I sensed he wanted to end the conversation.

"Thanks," I said, testing my ankle.

"Need some help getting home?"

"No, I'm go—" I cut myself off. What was I thinking? "Actually, I probably shouldn't put too much weight on it right away."

He put his arm around my waist and pulled me snug against his side. With my arm draped over his shoulder, I whimpered periodically as he helped me hobble home. Maybe the Oscar was in *my* future.

"Okay then, later," he said.

"Yeah, later. And thanks." Once inside, I leaned my back against the door and just enjoyed the moment. But then my mind drifted to the events prior to my tumble. I was puzzled, no, more like intrigued. I thought about everything Megan and Sam had said. I wondered how many times they'd had to give that same explanation, to how many people. Mostly, I wondered if they believed it.

You think your family's so weird until you observe someone else's. And that's exactly what I was going to do. Somehow I was going to find out what was going on over there.

chapter

M egan and I were sitting on her front step, a jar of
peanut butter between my feet, a box of Ritz crackers
between Megan's.

"You're not doing it right," I said. "You have to have at least
five in your stack." I demonstrated my building process then
showed her how I could still easily fit my mouth around it.

She looked at me doubtfully, brushing away some of my
cracker debris that landed on her arm. "I think I'll just do
two."

"Well *that's* not very exciting," I joked.

I was sharing my breakfast with Megan. I had noticed her
sitting on the porch with Peter, the cat. Violin music was
coming from the house so I knew Sam was practicing. The
van wasn't in the driveway. She looked sort of lonely so I had
made my way across the street, bringing my feast with me.

"Oh. How's the job going?" Megan asked, nibbling
delicately on a cracker.

My mouth was jammed full so I had to finish chewing first. "You know, it's actually okay. Dad doesn't treat me like his little girl and everyone in the office is really nice. So yeah. Better than I thought."

I shook the box. There were only a few crackers left. I held the box out to Megan.

She put up her hands in protest and shook her head.

"When's your mom back?" I asked, rolling the bag down inside the cracker box.

"I don't know. I think she's scoping out spots for photos."

"Come over and hang out then," I said excitedly.

"Can't. Mom doesn't like us to go anywhere when she's not home, and we're not allowed any visitors." She looked at me out of the corner of her eye.

"Oh…okay." I tried to make my voice sound as though I didn't think that was totally weird.

We sat quietly, both still flicking away stray shards of cracker.

There was an odd sound I couldn't place.

Megan glanced back behind her. She rolled her eyes and shook her head.

I turned to see what was up. Sam was standing in the doorway with his mouth pressed up against the screen door, blowing out his cheeks, making fish faces. I rolled my eyes too and turned back around, pretending to ignore him. Of course, I really wanted him to join us. I wished I hadn't chowed down so enthusiastically on those crackers—I could have offered him some. I heard one last puff, then footsteps walking away. *That's what I get for being a little piggy.*

"He can be so...immature," Megan said, but she was smiling.

I grinned at her word choice. *Immature.* It was as if she couldn't come up with anything nastier than that to say about her brother. Now if that had been Jilly, I wouldn't have been able to get the word *moron* out of my mouth fast enough.

They were definitely close, way closer than me and Jilly. I had picked up on that the very first time I met them. They seemed to genuinely like each other, and they *never* fought. God, they probably even cared about each other's feelings. I concentrated hard on that for a second, trying to imagine what that must be like. I couldn't quite get there.

"He's my best friend, you know," Megan said quietly, as if she had been reading my thoughts.

I couldn't think how to respond so I just fiddled with my earring and nodded.

"That probably sounds strange to you," she continued.

"No," I lied. It did sound strange, but I sort of understood. They moved so much, spent so much time together, they were pretty much all each other had. "He's awfully nice to you, for a brother," I added.

"He really is," she nodded.

"I always wanted an older brother," I sighed.

We were soon distracted by a new noise, this time coming from the front of my house. I watched as Dad used the garden hose to fill a bucket. He held out a sponge to Jilly. He was trying to get her to wash the car. *Good luck with that.* Jilly stood there, arms folded, major frown on. The only thing missing was the defiant foot stomp. *Wait for it…and there it is.*

I turned to Megan. "Did I mention how I always wanted an older brother?"

She laughed and we entertained ourselves for the next little while watching Jilly attempt to wash the car. She kept her body as far away from the car as possible, leaning in and basically patting the car with the soapy sponge as though she was terrified of breaking a nail or something. Dad sat on our stone wall just shaking his head.

Now I was kind of relieved that Sam wasn't with us. Had Jilly seen him, she probably would have dumped the bucket over herself, going for the wet T-shirt effect.

"Okay, Jilly, thanks for your…er…help. You can go now," I heard Dad announce. I guess he couldn't take it anymore.

"Thanks, Daddy," Jilly squealed as she dropped the sponge and ran.

"Can you believe that?" I said to Megan. "I mean, why does he let her get away with crap like that?"

"That's what dads do," she said wistfully.

I shrugged.

"You're so lucky. Your dad seems awesome. I can just tell."

Her voice was barely more than a whisper. "You know how they say you can't miss something you never had?"

"Yeah."

"I don't think that's true about everything, at least about a dad." There was a sadness in her voice that I could actually feel.

From what Megan had just said, I concluded she didn't see her dad much…or maybe ever. "How often do you see yours?" I asked.

"Never."

I swallowed. "Never? Is he…alive?"

"I don't know for sure."

"You don't know? How can you not know?" As soon as the words were out I regretted them. They came across harsher than I meant. Plus, I didn't want her to think I was being nosey. But she had never talked about her dad before, and I wanted to take advantage of the moment.

"I've never seen him. Not even a picture." She was in a kind of trance, staring off at something far away.

I hesitated, but only for a second. "You mean you don't know anything about him? Nothing?"

"Nothing."

"But why?" I was now beyond nosey.

She turned and looked at me. Her eyes were teary. "She won't tell us anything, she won't even let us ask." Her voice became more intense. "I don't even know his name."

Trying to imagine how she felt was impossible—not to know your own dad, anything about him, if he was even alive. I sat quietly trying to think of something helpful to say, something to make her feel better.

At the same time, I listened to Dad yelp out a string of obscenities after he put his foot in the bucket of soapy water. He wasn't what I'd call graceful, but at least he was all mine.

I heard her sniff beside me. I felt bad that she was upset and wished I'd shut my mouth and hadn't kept asking her questions.

"Dad's dropping me and Jilly at the mall later," I said, attempting to lighten the mood. "Wanna come with us?"

"Um…well, my mom's not back yet so…"

"We're not going till after lunch. She might be back by then."

"I don't think she'll let me." She didn't bother making an excuse.

I sighed. "Well, don't forget to ask about going to the waterfront. She *can't* not let you do that, it practically borders on educational."

"Maybe." She closed her eyes and rubbed her forehead like she was in pain.

"You okay? I'm sorry if I was being pushy." I decided I'd harassed her enough for one day.

"No, you're not being pushy," she assured me. "I'm just tired. I haven't been sleeping much. My mom—" She stopped.

"Yeah…your mom…?" For some reason I felt it was very important that she finish that sentence. I noticed she was sliding her ring up and down her finger again. I had seen her do that before, mostly when she seemed nervous.

She took a deep breath. "My mom says it's just because I'm not used to the new house yet."

"Right, of course," I nodded, knowing that wasn't what she had been going to say at all.

Standing up, I brushed off more crumbs and gathered up my cracker box and peanut butter. "I should really go help Dad. He's still struggling over there."

"Thanks for sharing your breakfast." She smiled up at me, shielding her eyes from the sun. She seemed to be herself again.

"Thanks for the company." I smiled back.

I slowly walked to my driveway, organizing all the pieces of information I'd learned into categories in my brain. Scrunching up my forehead, I wondered if I was going to need some kind of flow chart or diagram to help me keep all this stuff straight so I could eventually connect the dots.

I stopped by our car. Dad's sopping wet sport sock was hanging from the garden trellis. "Want some help, Dad?"

"Thanks, Pumpkin, but I think I'm almost done here."

I turned as the Swickers' van pulled into their driveway. I wondered if Megan would ask about going to the mall. I saw Megan say something to Mrs. Swicker. Mrs. Swicker waved her hands in the air and continued into the house. Megan's eyes met mine and she slowly shook her head. I gave her a sympathetic nod. "Maybe next time," I said, but I don't think she heard me.

chapter

7

Departure time for the mall was 1:30 PM, not a minute before or a minute after. Being on time was something Dad was very strict about. No wiggle room whatsoever. More than once he'd left me or Jilly standing in the driveway as he pulled away because we weren't ready. He only drove around the block, he'd always come back to get us, and I know he was just teaching us a lesson, but it's still kind of traumatic, especially when you're *five*! It was pretty funny whenever he did it to Jilly, though.

Dad was holding open the car door. "Let's bust a move, as you kids like to say."

Jilly and I looked at each other.

"We don't say that, Dad," I said, sliding into the car.

"*Nobody* says that," Jilly added dryly.

When we arrived at the mall, Jilly and I slowly wove our way in and out of the stores and boutiques. My shopping was totally off. The force just wasn't with me. I couldn't concentrate. I was suffering from Swickeritis, it was infecting every part of me. I ended up buying a T-shirt that I didn't even like from the Gap. Jilly talked me into it, I suspected because she wanted to borrow it.

We picked through a basket of discounted jewelry.

"Your new T-shirt would look great with my yoga pants, the Lulu Lemons—you know, because of the yellow around the waist," Jilly said casually.

I knew it! "Are you offering to lend me your pants?"

"Uh…no." She tilted her head and gave me an apologetic look. "They're kind of my *favourite*. Vivian and I are going to Nubody's tonight. I thought maybe I could borrow the shirt…to, you know…wear with the pants."

"I don't *think* so." Then it dawned on me, what she'd just said. "Nubody's!" I laughed. "Since when do *you* work out?"

"Hey!" she exclaimed, all offended. "I like to stay in shape!"

I shook my head, still laughing. There had to be a boy, or boys, involved. They either worked there, or worked out there. I'd love to see Jilly attempting some kind of physical activity—she has to take a nap after vacuuming.

She wound a rainbow-coloured necklace of beads around my neck and stood back to see how they looked. "I'm thinking about asking Sam out," she announced out of the blue.

I started to cough, choking on something that had suddenly formed in my throat.

Jilly slapped me on the back, and not very gently either.

"Better?"

Nodding, I swallowed the mystery glob. "I dunno about Sam, Jilly. I mean, all he does is practice his violin. I don't think he's really into all that." I hoped I sounded more confident than I felt.

"Oh come on, Lid," she said, stretching out her arm to critique a bracelet she'd slipped on. "He's got to wanna have fun *sometimes*."

I stood and watched her try on bracelet after bracelet, necklace after necklace, waiting for the imaginary devil horns that had sprouted on her head to fade away. It took longer than usual this time.

"And the name is Lydia, not Lid," I finally said between clenched teeth as she dragged me next door to the Laura Secord ice cream shop. So much for staying in shape.

She ordered for me—I was too deep in thought trying to come up with a persuasive argument that might keep her away from Sam. She handed me a Supreme something or other. It was just okay. The fact that it cost almost as much as my T-shirt kind of took away from the flavour.

We met up with Dad at the assigned time. I sat in the back so I could sulk in private. Jilly was going to ask Sam out. And of course he was going to say yes. I closed my eyes, focusing all my energy on Jilly, wondering if maybe I could put a mild curse on her or something. Like if she would come down with a *smallish* illness, nothing life-threatening, just potent enough to put her out of action for a couple weeks. I opened one eye. She still looked fine to me.

I sat up a little straighter as we pulled into the driveway. Sam and Megan were leaning on their porch rail. They both looked up when they heard our car doors slam, and began to walk towards the street, motioning for me to come. I met them halfway.

"We can go," Megan said.

"Go?" I wasn't sure what she was talking about.

"Your waterfront tour thing, we can go," Sam explained.

"*Really?*" I didn't bother to hide my surprise. "That's great!"

"Yeah, it *is* great." Megan looked kind of surprised herself. "We can work it all out later. I just wanted to let you know."

"Sure," I nodded.

I watched them go back inside, while I stood in the middle of the street clutching the plastic bag with my gaudy T-shirt inside. I tried to imagine the conversation that must have gone on between them and Mrs. Swicker while I was at the mall. Whatever it was, it worked. If someone had asked me if I thought they'd be allowed to go out for a whole day with *me*, I'd stake all 307 dollars in my savings account on the answer being no.

My mouth broke into a satisfied smile. I was glad I was wrong. It gets boring being right all the time.

chapter

8

I couldn't believe it. Not sure what I couldn't believe more,
the fact that our downtown expedition finally came
together, or that their freak show of a mother was coming
with us.

See, when Mrs. Swicker gave them the green light to
go on the condition that she take us, I was under the crazy
impression that she was offering to drive us down and pick
us up. I actually thought, Hey, what a team player, anything's
better than the bus. But *noooo*, she meant she was staying with
us for the whole time, the *whole* time.

I almost called it off when Sam and Megan explained it to
me. I begged Mom to talk Mrs. Swicker into letting us go on
our own. But she said Mrs. Swicker probably wanted to see
the sights too. For some reason she just wouldn't believe me
when I told her Mrs. Swicker was some kind of alien being
sent to earth to wreak havoc. She had the nerve to say I was
overreacting.

I think Sam and Megan sensed my disappointment. They had looked at me with a kind of pleading expression in their eyes. I couldn't back out. Secretly I fantasized, hoped they were planning on making a break for it, hiding away on the closest yacht or cruise ship that happened to be tied up, declaring immunity or whatever it was you did when you defected to another country. I wasn't going to be the one to muck up their escape plans.

Finally realizing it was Mrs. Swicker's way or no way, I decided to suck it up and stay positive, even if it killed me.

I usually worked Monday, Wednesday, and Friday, so I suggested a Tuesday, a weekday, explaining that the weekends were just too crowded. Real reason? Jilly would be babysitting, and I knew Mom would want me to include her if we went on a Saturday or Sunday. Except for the Mrs. Swicker thing, everything was coming together just as I'd planned, me and Sam would walk along the boardwalk, take in the sights, gaze out over the ocean…oh yeah, and Megan too.

The Swickers' van came to a stop as we got closer to the downtown core.

"I thought you said it wouldn't be that crowded on a weekday," Mrs. Swicker said, real snarky.

"Well, I really meant *less* crowded," I responded sweetly.

"Humph."

I glanced out the front window. The cars were stopped because the light was *red*. I had to press my lips together to keep myself from pointing this out. There was just something about this woman that made me want to pick a fight every single time.

We were moving again. I instructed everyone to keep their eyes open for a parking meter. We had to circle the block a couple times. I could tell Mrs. Swicker was getting crankier with every corner turned. Megan and I erupted into screams when we saw a convertible pull out of a spot.

"There, Mom, there!" Megan pointed wildly.

Mrs. Swicker hushed us and parallel parked the van.

As we made our way down the hill towards the waterfront, I tried to stay upbeat and enthusiastic, pointing out historical buildings and stuff like that. I *really* felt like we were out on a day pass with our probation officer.

Sam and Megan seemed to find everything interesting. Mrs. Swicker didn't comment one way or the other, which was fine by me.

I pointed out a giant display all about the *Bluenose* and Sam and Megan pressed their faces to the glass, soaking up every word.

"Lydia. Where can I get a coffee?" Mrs. Swicker snapped impatiently.

Wordlessly, I raised my arm and pointed to a nearby coffee stand.

About to make my way over to Sam and Megan, I stopped. Mrs. Swicker was dumping packets of sugar into her coffee, but that wasn't all. I watched as she looked around, pulled something silver out of her purse, unscrewed the top, and quickly dumped it in her coffee.

I pretended I didn't notice anything unusual, like what was I going to say? So when Mrs. Swicker re-joined us, I continued giving them the grand tour. We started at one end of the boardwalk, stopping to check out various sail boats and even a couple of private yachts. We poked in and out of shops and stopped for ice cream. At the other end of the boardwalk was the museum. I loved going there, especially the section devoted to the *Titanic*. I had a bit of an obsession with that disaster and I blathered on until I noticed Sam and Megan's eyes glazing over. Mrs. Swicker looked like she was having a cavity filled.

I wanted to end at my favourite store. It was a gift shop filled with everything Nova Scotian.

"Here it is. You'll love this place," I said.

Walking through the door, we were hit in the face with wonderful gift shop smells: soaps, candles, maple fudge. It was heavenly. I stood in the centre of the store, taking a moment to just breathe it all in. Sam and Megan immediately gravitated to a table covered with candies, fudge, and anything else that could possibly be made from maple sugar. Even Mrs. Swicker seemed to have found something of interest at a display in a far corner of the store.

I could never quite figure out what it was about these touristy gift shops that somehow made me have no issue whatsoever with forking over $12.95 plus tax for a bagpiper Christmas ornament that was basically made out of an old-fashioned clothespin, a black pompom, and a scrap of Nova Scotia tartan. They must put something in those scented candles. I wondered if mind control had a smell.

"Would you like your ornament in a gift box?" the clerk asked me.

"You bet," I said, determined to get my money's worth one way or another.

Everyone else was still busy looking around, so I wandered over to look at a case of pewter charms.

There seemed to be a flood of new people into the shop. I knew there was a cruise ship in. We'd seen part of it from the boardwalk. They all looked fresh off the promenade deck. Big floppy hats, big sunglasses, big American accents. I craned my neck to check on Sam and Megan.

Megan was standing on her tippy toes, waving a giant stuffed lobster at me. I gave her a thumbs up.

The noise level inside the tiny shop seemed to be increasing. I thought about waiting outside, but a nearby shriek grabbed my attention.

"Reenie? Reenie Barretto? I can't believe it!"

The voice came booming out of a large, sunburnt, bejewelled platinum blonde. The intriguing bit was that she seemed to be directing her outburst towards Mrs. Swicker.

I repositioned myself, stepping behind a spinning rack of Maritime cookbooks so I could watch the scene unobserved.

The blonde stepped closer to Mrs. Swicker and tried again. "Reenie! It's me, Phyllis!"

My eyes darted to Mrs. Swicker. I saw her back stiffen, and her face turned almost grey. It was just like in a book, when it says, "the colour drained from her face." It was *just* like that. She acted as though she couldn't hear the woman and didn't look up from the soap display.

The blonde reached out and put her hand on Mrs. Swicker's arm as if to turn her around.

I held my breath. This was getting good. I actually hissed "*Move!*" to a tourist who wanted to look through my cookbook rack.

"Remember? Coral High? Same homeroom? Mr. Simmons, the crazy suspenders?" The blonde was not giving up.

My eyes flew back to Mrs. Swicker. I watched as she took a deep breath, pressed her lips together, and slowly turned around. Her hands were shaking slightly as she lifted the woman's hand off her arm and let it drop as though it was something infected. "I'm sorry," she said. "You must have me confused with someone else."

The blonde began poking herself in the chest. "It's me, Phyllis Gregory, of course now Phyllis Munroe." Poke, poke. "Can you believe I married Jerry after all the miserable things

61

I called him? Remember the three of us smoking Kools under the bleachers?" Poke, poke.

I frantically looked around for Sam and Megan. I couldn't believe they were missing all this. They were way over on the other side, a sea of people between us.

"Like I said, you have me confused with someone else," Mrs. Swicker said coldly.

The blonde must have finally picked up on something in her voice. She took a step backwards. "Pardon me, I guess I have. You look exactly like a girl I used to go to school with." The blonde tilted her head as she spoke, as if maybe she wasn't so sure anymore. "Sorry to have bothered you."

Mrs. Swicker ignored the blonde's apology. Her eyes swept the shop and landed on me, still hiding behind the rack. I blinked and quickly looked away, making like I was flipping through the cookbooks. She picked up a couple of soaps and headed for the cash.

I stayed in my hiding spot for a minute, chewing on my fingernail. *That was more than a little interesting.* Too bad Sam and Megan hadn't seen it. I still didn't really know what to make of it. I wondered if Mrs. Swicker would say anything. Maybe not, if she didn't think anyone saw. She must know I saw at least some of it. Of course, it may have been totally legit, just an innocent case of mistaken identity. And maybe Mrs. Swicker's reaction was just because that big, loud, blonde woman freaked her out. She *was* kind of overwhelming...Nope. No matter how I tried spin it, I just couldn't convince myself. It was all way too bizarre.

The crowd in the store thinned. We finished our shopping and met up outside.

"That was actually pretty all right, as far as shopping goes," Sam said.

"Oh yeah? What'd ya get?" I asked.

"This book on Maritime history, and this other one on local ghost stories. Oh, and I blew eight dollars on fudge."

"Impressive. What'd you get, Megan?"

"I had to have this lobster. That pretty much drained me of all my cash."

I turned to Mrs. Swicker, determined not to let on that I had seen the exchange in the gift shop. I plastered on a smile. "And what did—"

"I'm going to that booth to grab some maps," she said, cutting me off.

We watched her walk away.

"I don't think she heard you," Megan said.

"No worries," I shrugged, not wanting them to feel uncomfortable. The way their mom acted wasn't *their* fault.

"What'd *you* get?" Sam asked. I got the feeling he was trying to divert my attention.

"Oh. I got this wicked ornament." I dug it out of its gift box. "See, it's a bagpiper." I flashed it quickly, my thumb

covering the price tag, then jammed it back in the bag.
$12.95…I must be nuts.

Mrs. Swicker came back from the booth with a handful of
maps and another coffee. I wondered what she'd put in it *this*
time.

We began walking again. I glanced back over my shoulder,
checking that she was lurking at an acceptable distance, if
there was such a thing.

Sam unwrapped a piece of fudge and held it out to me.
"This place kind of reminds me of when we lived in Portland."

"Thanks." I took a bite of fudge. "Maine?"

"Yeah, but only for—"

"Are we all done here now?" Mrs. Swicker butted in.

I couldn't tell if she meant the tour or the conversation. I
decided both.

chapter
9

I was sitting on the end of my bed doing not much of anything except feeling sorry for myself. I had asked Sam and Megan to go swimming at Kearney Lake. Mom was going to drive us and everything. Mrs. Swicker wouldn't let them go. I know, big shocker. I seriously wanted to have it out with that woman, demand to know why she wouldn't let her kids go for a swim in this sweltering heat. It bordered on child abuse. Of course I didn't say a word. It was all just big talk, safe inside my head. But I was really starting to despise her, not to mention I was pretty sure she might have some kind of drinking problem.

Mom came into my room with a pile of clean laundry. "Special delivery," she sang.

"Yay," I mumbled.

"What's wrong, honey? You look like someone ran over your dog."

"You won't let us have a dog."

Mom sighed. "You know what I mean."

"Nothing's wrong."

She leaned against my desk and gave me a long look. After a minute she said, "I was thinking of inviting the Swickers over for a barbecue, let them meet some of the other neighbours. What do you think?"

"I dunno, could you somehow leave Mrs. Swicker out of the invite?"

"Well, that's highly unlikely."

"Then I don't think it's a good idea. They won't come anyways."

"Lydia, what *is* it with you and Mrs. Swicker?"

I didn't answer.

"Seriously, Lydia, what's the problem?" Mom persisted.

I picked at my fingernail, not meeting her eyes. "Mom, she's so…*mean!*"

"Has she been mean to you?" she demanded quickly.

"Yeah…well, no…not *mean* mean, more like *snarky* mean. But it's *more* than that…it's like there's something really, *really* creepy about her," I tried to explain.

"Lydia." She had that stern tone in her voice.

"Mom! You've got to trust me on this one. There's something not right about her. She's like something out of a horror flick."

Mom crossed her arms and shook her head sadly. It was as if she had just realized she would now have to keep all her weekends free so she could visit me in the institution. "Lydia, I think it would be wise to let this go," she said, reaching for the door.

"I know I'm right about this," I said stubbornly.

She turned slowly, drilling her eyes into me, her lips pinched together.

No words were spoken. There didn't have to be. I knew all too well what that look meant: *Watch it.*

I almost told her about Mrs. Swicker dumping stuff in her coffee, but I figured she'd just say it was probably some nonfat dairy creamer substitute. Jeez, it couldn't have been that, could it? No, not a chance.

"Go ahead! Invite away!" I hollered after she left. "They're not going to come!"

No response. I knew I'd end up paying for that smartass remark somewhere down the road.

I got up to close my door. I was about to slam it then wised up at the last moment.

Of course I should have known better. I sat in my chair and slumped forward over my desk, my head resting on my arms. I mean, it's not that hard. I'm smart enough to know what to say and what not to say, to stay out of trouble, come in just under the radar, keep the 'rents happy. So why didn't I just do it? *Argh!*

Whenever Mom was ticked at me, I always ended up with a sick feeling, like some tiny parasite was eating the lining of my stomach. I decided I might as well just get it over with and go apologize.

The door to Mom's office was slightly ajar. About to knock,

I realized she was talking on the phone. The word "barbecue" floated through the air. I held my breath and pushed my back flat against the wall, inching my ear closer to the door. Not that I was an eavesdropper. Not like Mrs. Swicker, who made it part of her daily routine. I only encouraged it in very extreme circumstances. Was this one of those circumstances? I wouldn't really be able to make a fair ruling until after I heard the conversation.

"Well, it would just be a few neighbours from the street," I heard Mom say.

Pause.

"Really, you wouldn't have to do or bring a thing." Mom was using her most persuasive voice.

Pause.

"Oh. Well, okay…I understand." I could tell by her tone that she didn't. "Maybe some other time." In fact, I'd have to say she sounded a little put out.

Feeling rather pleased with myself and totally vindicated, I quietly tiptoed back to my room. Maybe I wouldn't apologize after all. Maybe I'd wait for the apology to come to me.

chapter

Jilly sashayed into the kitchen looking like the cat that swallowed the canary.

I ignored her and kept focusing on my Sudoku.

She sat down across from me and started humming, really loudly, not to mention out of tune. I could tell she was just *dying* for me to ask her what was up. It was bad enough the Darcys had let her have the day off *with pay*. There was no way I was giving her the satisfaction. I kept my eyes down, concentrating doubly hard on my puzzle. I lasted about a minute and a half. The non-musicalness that ran in our family had hit Jilly the hardest. I slammed down my pencil.

"You win. What's up?"

She leaned across the table, checked behind both her shoulders (don't ask me who she thought was watching her) and whispered, "I asked Sam to a movie."

"You did what?" My voice was so high-pitched, I sounded like a chipmunk.

"I asked Sam to a movie."

"Oh my God," I said, mostly to myself. My ears were ringing and my vision blurred. I was beginning to think I was having an aneurism right on the spot. "What do you mean you asked him to a movie?"

"What do you mean, what do I mean?"

"And he said *yes*?"

"Well…*yeah*."

"And he's *allowed*?"

"I guess."

I took a calming breath, turned, and marched out of the kitchen, head held high. Once in the privacy of my own room, I looked around for something to smash, throw, damage in some way. Huh! That wasn't too bright, this was all *my* stuff. I should have gone into Jilly's room.

Plunking myself down on my bed, I picked at my chipped fingernail polish. A movie was dangerous. At a movie, they'd be alone in the dark. I began calculating some kind of revenge. Blue dye in her shampoo bottle? Saw it on a TV show once. I sighed. They'd trace it back to me right away. I knew I was being overly dramatic and childish about the whole thing. This was so not like me. Until now, I've never been that jealous of Jilly. To be honest, most days I feel pretty superior to her. She really has mastered that whole *blonde thing* though. Actually, most people say we look a lot alike. She just seems to know how to work it better than me.

I brushed the flecks of nail polish onto the floor. Things were definitely going from bad to worse. Mom was all over me about Mrs. Swicker, and now…Jilly and Sam.

Feeling in a bit of a funk, I thought I might walk to the drug store and buy a new nail polish or a fashion mag to cheer myself up. It was a very Jilly thing to do, but as much as I hated to admit it, it had worked for me in the past.

I stood on the front step digging around in my pocket to make sure I had enough money. There was something going on in front of the Swickers'. I kept my head down pretending to count out my change, but my eyeballs were rolled up as far as they could go. From what I could see, Megan and Mrs. Swicker were arguing. I was kind of surprised that they were so loud. They obviously didn't see me. I tried to creep up the driveway a little, hoping to hear something. Megan seemed to be trying to walk away. My eyes popped out of my head when I saw Mrs. Swicker grab her arm and yank her back.

"Hey, Megan!" I shouted.

Mrs. Swicker quickly let go of Megan's arm.

Megan looked up and waved me over.

I crossed the street, what else could I do?

"I'll just give her my key, Mom. It's just for one night," Megan said under her breath, then she turned to me. "We have to go away overnight. Poor Peter has a kidney infection and I was wondering if you would feed him and give him his medicine."

"Sure," I shrugged.

"It's not necessary, Lydia," Mrs. Swicker said coldly. "We'll just leave some food out on the back step."

I half expected her to say, "We're just going to have him put down."

"Mom." There were tears forming in Megan's eyes. "What about his medicine? He shouldn't be out all night when he's sick."

It was at that moment my mom arrived on the scene. "Hello, Bernadette, Megan. Sorry to interrupt, but Lydia... don't forget you've got the dentist at four. Dad's coming home for an early lunch." She leaned towards Mrs. Swicker and put her hand on her arm. "He's doing low-carb and finds it easier to eat at home," she explained in a hushed voice.

I choked back a laugh—as if Mrs. Swicker would give a crap.

"He'll take you back with him," Mom told me, "and you can work until I pick you up."

"Okay...umm...Mom?" I was hoping her presence might cause that mysterious shift again. "Megan was just asking me to look after Peter while they were away."

"Oh, that shouldn't be a problem."

Mrs. Swicker pressed her lips together. "As I told Lydia, if we leave some food out, Peter will be just—"

"Oh, don't be silly, Bernadette, we're right here, it's no trouble." Mom waved a hand in the air.

Mrs. Swicker looked stung, like someone had just slapped her in the face. My guess, being called silly was a whole new experience for her.

It occurred to me, this was probably the first time Mom and Mrs. Swicker had seen each other since the great barbecue blow-off of '09. There was a kind of bizarre showdown feeling in the air. Which also reminded me, I was still waiting for that apology.

Mom started to root around in her purse. "You know, Bernadette," she continued, "we really should exchange house keys anyways. It's good for when the kids get locked out and things like that."

My eyes darted back and forth between the two women. Mrs. Swicker looked like she was praying for death. I suspected Mom sensed all the weirdness, but she pretended everything was normal.

Mom was still going through her purse. "Darn. I thought I had an extra key in here…Oh well…" She looked up. "So you want Lydia to feed Peter just the one night then?"

Mrs. Swicker opened her mouth to protest but then closed it. I knew she had nothing.

"Just tonight and again tomorrow morning," Megan answered. "Sam has a chance to have a private session with Wolfgang Snitzel, the world famous violinist," her voice filled with pride. "We'll be back later tomorrow."

"Hey…why don't you just stay here, you could sleep over," I said.

Megan turned and looked up at her mother with wide, pleading eyes.

"We'd love to have her," Mom added.

Mrs. Swicker's face froze in a thin smile. "Thank you, Justine, but I would really like Megan to come. I think she could benefit from the experience. She has a bit of musical talent herself."

Megan and I both sighed with disappointment. Mom had won the first round. I guess it was too much to hope for that she'd stick it to Mrs. Swicker two times in a row.

Mom put her hand on Megan's shoulder. "Don't worry, sweetie, we'll have you for a sleepover another time."

Megan smiled up at her.

Mrs. Swicker began to tap her foot impatiently. "Megan, you should get your things packed."

"Okay," Megan said. "I'll write everything down, Lydia, and bring it over to you. It'll be real easy."

Megan arrived on my doorstep a few minutes later with her key and all the instructions for Peter. I told her not to worry, to have a good time and I'd see her when she got back. Putting her note and key in my night-table drawer, I stood in my room trying to remember what I was doing before all this happened. Oh yeah. Jilly's big date, nail polish.

I heard the telephone and glanced at my princess phone, watching it light up with each ring. I wasn't in the mood to answer it. The ringing stopped. I listened. Not for me.

A minute later there was a swish of blonde hair as Jilly leaned sideways across my doorway.

"What do you want?" I grumbled.

"Well…since you seemed so *interested* in my date, thought you'd like to know that it's off."

My heart skipped a beat. "What do you mean?"

"For God's sake, Lid, would you quit asking me that question? You're such a pinhead. What do you think I mean?"

"I just wanted to know why it's off." I tried to make my voice sound sincere, like I was concerned about how she felt. It was totally draining.

She sighed. "His mom won't let him go."

"Really?" *You don't say.*

"Yeah. Apparently he has some kind of violin thing. Can you believe that?"

"A violin thing, huh?"

"Totally lame. Falls into the same category as 'I have to wash my hair.'" Her eyes widened. "You don't think he just made it up, do you?"

The little devil on my shoulder encouraged me to nurture Jilly's paranoia, but I couldn't do it. "No. He really does have a violin thing. But I think it's probably more that his mom won't let him," I added.

"It was only a movie."

"The mom's a major head case. She doesn't let them do *anything.* I wanted Megan to go to the mall the other day and her mom wouldn't let her. I don't think she even bothers to give them a reason."

"Seriously? Ouch. I'd literally *die* if I couldn't go to the mall."

And so ended our almost intelligent conversation. "Ummm, maybe you should think about looking for some kind of support group for that."

"Oh. You're soooo funny, Lid."

"Stop calling me that, you know I hate it," I hissed.

"Well it's better than Jarhead. Get it? Lid, Jarhead, a lid's a top for a jar. I just thought that up! I *kill* me."

"Yeah, you're a comic genius. Now get out."

She flicked her hair and left my room.

Thank God.

I smiled to myself as I flapped my arms through the air, trying to get rid of Jilly's strawberry shampoo smell. So...the date was off. I should have known better than to let myself get so worked up about it. Deep down I knew there was no way Mrs. Swicker would have ever let it happen. She wouldn't let them do anything that took them out of her sight.

Look at all the hassle over the trip to the waterfront. Talk about brutal. And then there was the scene in the gift shop. Still hadn't come up with an explanation for that one. There seemed to be no end to this woman's weirdness.

I went to my desk, checking to see where I had scribbled it on my notepad. There it was, *Reenie Barretto*. That was the

name the woman had called her. I had written it down as
soon as I'd gotten home that day. I don't know why, I just did.

chapter

11

"Peter! Here, Peter, Peter, Peter!" I shook the little bell on the key chain just like Megan had told me to. The cat immediately appeared from between the bushes and did a figure eight in and around my ankles. He meowed loudly while I fumbled with the keys.

As I swung open the door, Peter leapt inside ahead of me. I reached for the light switch. Even though it was still daytime, the house was kind of dark. It was cold inside. I hugged my arms around myself. I sniffed. The house smelled... disinfected.

I thought I'd take my time today. Last night when I'd fed Peter, I was in a rush. Mom had offered to take me to a movie at the last minute so I was in and out pretty quickly. Peter was probably lonely and wanting some company. I felt nervous being alone in the house and I wasn't sure why. It sort of felt like I'd just broken in or something. I knew I should just feed the cat and leave, but I couldn't do it. The opportunity to do a little light snooping was way too good to pass up.

Standing in the middle of the family room, I turned slowly, taking in the details, looking for something…but what? There was not one thing out of place, no sofa cushion un-fluffed, not one speck of dust on the furniture.

I moved into the kitchen. It was spotless just like I knew it would be. The house looked as though no one lived in it. I shivered and rubbed my arms again.

My destination was Mrs. Swicker's room. I used to babysit for the Henleys, so I knew the layout of the house. I tiptoed down the hall to the master bedroom. I felt it was necessary to tiptoe for some reason. The room was pretty much how I remembered, which was disappointing. I think I was expecting to see a coffin or something instead of a bed, though I suppose she *could* have slept hanging upside down in the closet. There were no personal items anywhere, not even a photo. Come to think of it, there didn't seem to be anything like that anywhere in the house. Maybe that's why it felt so cold and…creepy. I had an overwhelming urge to go through her dresser drawers, but I stopped myself and backed out of the room without touching a thing.

I peeked in Sam's room. It was neat as a pin. I sat on his bed, looked around to soak things up a bit, see if I could actually learn anything about him. The books he'd bought at the gift shop were on his nightstand. The paperback covers were curled upwards, so he must have been reading them.

I stood up, smoothed the bedspread, and went over to scope out his desk. There was a huge stack of sheet music. I flicked through the papers hoping maybe I'd find "Sam + Lydia" doodled in the margins. No such luck. The music and the books were the only things that really told me this room was Sam's. I did a final check to make sure everything was the way I had found it.

It was the same in Megan's room, the neatness. I smiled at the giant lobster on her bed. For some reason I'd thought her room would be messier. I think that was because I considered her to be the most normal of the bunch. Sam was the unattainable beautiful boy, and Mrs. Swicker…well…I wasn't quite sure *what* she was.

I took another quick tour of the main floor. There wasn't even any mail piled on the hall table. If they had to, they could easily be packed up and gone in about five minutes.

Peter found me. He stood at my feet and purred, but I could see the accusation in his eyes.

"You're right, I should be feeding you. Let's do this," I said.

I thought about Mrs. Swicker as I crushed up Peter's pill and stirred it into his Meow Mix. Thought about how she'd react if she could see me nosing around her house. I pictured her head slowly blowing up like a balloon until it exploded and sent bits of brain matter flying and splat, dripping down the walls.

There was a jug by the sink. I filled it and carried it over to top up Peter's water bowl. My mouth suddenly went dry.

What if Mrs. Swicker had some kind of camera thing set up in here? It would totally be like something she'd do. My eyes raced around the room, along the edges of the ceiling. Nothing. I gave myself a mental slap in the head.

Unfortunately, during my little panic attack, I forgot to stop pouring the water into Peter's bowl.

Crap! I ran to the counter looking for something to soak up the mess. I returned to the scene of the accident dragging about fifty sheets of Bounty behind me.

Double crap! It was worse than I'd thought. The spilled water had basically disappeared. This was not a good thing. The water had leaked down between the boards of the hardwood floor.

Last summer, I overwatered Mom's palm tree in our dining room. The water leaked through the hardwood floor and stained the ceiling tiles downstairs in our family room. Apparently those tiles had been discontinued a thousand years ago. Dad was all for replacing the damaged ones with ones that were close enough, but Mom almost went into cardiac arrest over *that* idea. They fought for almost a week. I began to wonder who was going to get stuck with Jilly in the divorce. In the end some kind of compromise was reached. Mom got her new ceiling. I can't remember what Dad got, but I think it involved golf.

There was barely enough water to mop up. Sitting back on my heels, I contemplated my next move. I knew I had to go downstairs and check out whether or not I'd done any damage. I took the sheets of paper towel with me.

Downstairs, I figured it had to be the furnace room or garage that was directly under Peter's water bowl. And if they were like ours, there would be no real ceiling to stain.

I held my breath, opened the door, and flicked on the light. It was the furnace room. I looked up—just the wooden floorboards. I almost fainted with relief. The room was pretty much empty except for the furnace and a tower of boxes in the far corner. And then I heard it. The ping, ping of dripping water. Of course the water was leaking onto the boxes, where else? Just my luck.

Sighing, I made my way over to the pile. Lifting down the top box, I could tell by the dark colour of the cardboard that it was soaked. I carefully peeled back the packing tape, hoping to maintain some stickiness so I could re-tape the box and no one would be able to tell. I opened the soggy flaps, praying that I hadn't ruined anything important.

"Phew, just blankets."

I grabbed a stool from the hall and stood on top to wipe up the drips clinging to the ceiling. I tried to absorb the extra moisture by pressing some paper towels against the wood.

Kneeling down beside the box, I waved the flaps back and forth, in an attempt to dry them out. I touched the blankets. There were two, rolled up like cylinders, and they felt pretty damp.

I thought maybe I'd just shake them a bit, air-dry them. As I lifted the first one out, I could feel something hard in the middle. I unrolled the blanket, which was a solid blue on the outside with tiny blue bunnies on the other side. What I found inside was a silver rattle, one of those ones that look like a miniature dumbbell. I took out the other blanket. Pink on the outside, same pink bunnies on the inside, same silver rattle.

I sat there on the floor for a minute, arms crossed. I was kind of surprised. Mrs. Swicker didn't strike me as the sentimental type. Baby stuff was the last thing I expected to find.

A blanket in each hand, I twirled around the furnace room doing my best impression of a rhythmic gymnast performing an Olympic gold medal ribbon routine. Satisfied they were dry enough, I knelt to re-roll them and pack them away in the exact way I had found them. I picked up the rattle that had been inside the pink blanket. I could feel engraving under my fingers. Holding it up close to my face I read, *Amy Elizabeth, July 1, 1994.*

I frowned. Amy Elizabeth? Who the heck was that? It was at that moment I heard a noise. The furnace room was next to the garage. I could hear a car engine in the driveway. My heart jumped into my throat and I felt the air being sucked out of my lungs. *They must be back early!* They weren't supposed to be back until later! Frantically I bundled everything up as best I could, pressed down the tape, put the box back, jammed the wet paper towel in my pocket, and tore back up the stairs. I slid across the floor, as if I were sliding into home base, and came to a stop by Peter and his bowl of Meow Mix just as the Swickers walked in the door.

"Hi!" I blurted. I could feel the sweat trickling down my back. My heart was beating so loudly, I could swear they must have been able to hear it.

Mrs. Swicker stood in the doorway looking down at me, a startled expression on her face.

"I just got here," I explained, my voice unnaturally loud. "Peter seemed lonely, I thought I should stay with him for a few minutes, pet him, talk to him, that kind of thing." I knew I was rambling.

Suspicion was written all over Mrs. Swicker's face. "I couldn't figure out why the door was unlocked," she said slowly.

"Just little ol' me." I swallowed nervously and stood up. "Everything's fine here, just fine."

Megan stepped around Mrs. Swicker and scooped up Peter. "Did you miss us, boy? Thanks again, Lydia."

"Oh it was fine, everything's just fine," I squeaked. I had to get out of there. "Okay, well…see ya tomorrow." I squeezed between Mrs. Swicker and Sam and rushed out the door. I was in such a hurry, I almost didn't notice how cute Sam looked with his new haircut.

chapter

12

My heart was still racing when I got back home. I went directly to the bathroom and closed the door behind me. Sitting on the edge of the tub, I nervously rocked back and forth waiting for my breathing to return to normal. I squeezed my eyes shut, trying to remember if I had turned off the light in the furnace room. Mom had us trained so well, I was hoping I'd done it instinctively. I just couldn't remember.

Mrs. Swicker was barely civil to me *now*. I couldn't imagine how she'd treat me if she suspected me of going through her stuff. If she noticed the light was on, if she saw the box, she'd be able to tell right away. Ohmygod! Then she'd tell Mom, and take it from there...the possibilities were endless, and none of them good.

If this whole thing blew up, I had to have a plan, a reason why I had been down there. The truth? Always an option, I suppose. Think. I just needed a couple minutes to think, and I did some of my best thinking in the bathroom. It was a result of Mom's unconventional (I prefer the word *twisted*)

approach to parenting. Whenever Jilly or I would get in
trouble, the kind of trouble when most parents would send
their kid to their room, Mom sent us to the bathroom. "It's no
punishment being sent to your room these days," she would
say, "iPods, TVs, a *bed!*…that's no hardship. Wish someone
would send me to *my* room and make me stay there for an
hour." So, it was off to the bathroom for us, and let me just
say, sitting in the bathroom for an hour? Pretty boring, not
much else to do but…think.

Okay, so the truth may have been the way to go. I mean,
I hadn't done anything wrong. My issue was that I knew
no matter how I explained it, Mrs. Swicker wasn't going
to believe me. She'd be convinced I was up to something. I
wanted to shake myself and say, "What do I care what she
thinks? I can't stand the woman." And that was true. I really
did feel that way. But there was something else: Mrs. Swicker
kind of scared me. I think I was actually afraid of her.

And what about that rattle? The name—Amy Elizabeth.
Who was that? And the date—July 1, 1994. I was pretty
sure Megan had mentioned once her birthday was around
Christmas. Did Sam and Megan have a sister? Where was
she? And the other blanket and rattle. Who did those belong
to? It all kind of weirded me out. I massaged my temples. I
was starting to get a headache. Lucky for me, I was in the
bathroom. I popped a couple Advil and leaned against the
vanity.

There was an impatient knock on the bathroom door. "Yo! Did you fall in or what?"

Jilly. I decided not to answer her. It seemed to work. I heard her footsteps leaving.

I wondered what my odds were of ever getting back to that furnace room and that box, checking out the other rattle, seeing what else was in there. As I sat back down on the edge of the tub, I heard the tinkle of a bell. It was Megan's key chain in my pocket. A smile spread across my face. I wondered how long it would take for someone to realize I still had it. Could I hang on to it long enough to get back in their house? Would I have the guts to actually go? If they asked for it back, I could say I misplaced it or something. Yeah, that could work. Of course I would have to wait for the right opportunity. Obviously the house would have to be empty. Unfortunately that didn't seem to be very often.

There was a brief moment when I contemplated just asking Sam and Megan, asking them about the rattles and this Amy Elizabeth. I talked myself out of it. I couldn't picture myself bringing it up. It would totally look like I'd been snooping.

There was another knock at the door.

"Lid! Get out! I wanna use the bathroom."

"Just use the downstairs one, would ya?"

"No! I have to do my eyebrows and I need Mom's tweezers. God, I'm starting to look like I've been raised by wolves."

"Come back in five minutes. Is that too much to ask?"

"Holy crap, Lid! I'm not asking for a friggin' kidney. Get out of the bathroom!"

I knew I'd never get any peace now. "Fine!" I huffed, and stormed out. "And you're right! You do look like you've been raised by wolves!" I hollered just before I slammed my bedroom door.

chapter

13

We were sitting at Megan's kitchen table. It was one of the few times I had actually been allowed in the house. Mrs. Swicker had to be home. That was the rule. Counting in my head, not including the cake delivery and feeding Peter, this was only the third time I'd been in their house since they'd moved in. Mrs. Swicker was downstairs doing God knows what. Megan said laundry. My guess was trying to make contact with her home planet.

I'd just finished telling Megan about the big scandal at Dad's office. Kelley, the girl I was filling in for, had taken her vacation with some guy she'd met on an online dating site, and after just two days, they'd bolted to Vegas and got married.

She didn't seem to find the story as fascinating as I did. Actually, I wasn't even sure she'd been listening. "You okay?" I asked, noticing the dark circles under her eyes.

"Yeah. Just tired. Mom must have been having bad dreams

or something. She talked in her sleep all night," Megan said, avoiding eye contact. "Once I was awake, I couldn't seem to drift off again."

I stopped what I was doing, my Oreo-filled hand poised mid-dunk over a glass of milk. "*Really?*" I rolled this around in my head for a second. "So…like…could you make out what she was saying?"

Megan looked up. She was doing that thing with her ring again, sliding it up and down her finger. I could tell she was struggling with something, like she was wondering whether or not to confide in me. After a worried glance around the room, she leaned in real close and whispered, "Stuff like, 'You deserve it. You made me do it.'"

"Wow," I gasped. "Freaky."

"I know, and it's not the first time," she continued. "Sam's heard her too."

"I wonder what she was talking about," I said, mostly to myself.

"Not a clue. But Sam says she's had that same dream for ages. I only noticed it since we moved here. Guess my room is closer to hers in this house."

"What do *you* think it means?"

"It sounds like something bad, doesn't it?"

"Hmm…because it doesn't seem like just a dream, it seems like more of a nightmare."

"Yes, definitely a nightmare," Megan nodded. "Sometimes

she yells."

I knew the answer to this question already, but, "I don't suppose you asked her about it?"

"No."

I took a sip of my milk. With this new development, and the box in the furnace room, my brain was definitely nearing overload. "What if…" I began, thinking out loud. But then good sense kicked in.

"What if what? Tell me what you're thinking."

"Forget it, I'm probably way off."

"Lydia!"

"Okay…What if it has something to do with your dad? Like maybe the person she's talking about in her dream is him." I said it in a really tentative, "feeling out the topic" sort of way.

"You mean like she did something to him?"

"I dunno…Maybe?"

"Something bad, you mean," Megan said, narrowing her eyes.

I shrugged my shoulders. I had a sinking feeling I was going to regret ever opening my big mouth…*again*.

"You mean something really bad. Like she *killed* him or something," Megan accused. Her tone had definitely changed.

"No, no," I lied. "You're blowing it out of proportion, that's the *extreme* version." My voice was light, but she didn't buy it. I was back-pedalling, knowing I had gone one step too far.

"You're not a very good liar," she said in a tight voice.

I could feel my face turning red. My brain was screaming at me to shut up. Do you think for once I could just listen? No sir-ee. "But if you think about it, it could really explain a lot of things. The strange way she acts, those dreams. And, like, what's the deal with your dad anyways? She won't let you even ask a question about him? You have to admit, that's kind of weird."

"Maybe *he's* the one who did something bad."

I took my time answering. "Okay…guess that's possible." I doubted it though. "Still, she must know you guys are going to want to know about him. I mean, really, why won't she just tell you? Or make something up even? You have no reason not to believe her if she did. It's bizarre. You must think so too."

"Just because she acts weird, or isn't like *your* mom, doesn't mean she's a *murderer*." That last word, *murderer*, just kind of hung there, letters strung through the air.

The screaming in my head finally took over. "You're totally right," I said. "When you put it like that, I don't know what I was thinking." I knew exactly what I was thinking. It made perfect sense to *me*, but sometimes you just have to know when to quit.

"I think maybe you should go," she said quietly. "I've got some stuff I'm supposed to do."

I puffed out my cheeks and let the air leak out through

my mouth. I felt like I was being dismissed. I made my way towards the door, real slow, waiting for her to call me back. She didn't.

To be honest, Megan's reaction surprised me a bit. Their mother-daughter relationship had always seemed sort of strained. Guess you never really know how someone feels about their mom until you suggest that she might be a murderer. I'd have to remember that for the next time.

Back home I stomped in the front door, sulk mode on high.

Mom was on the phone and held up a hand to shush me before I could even open my mouth. My shoulders slumped, I sighed and leaned against the doorframe. After listening for a minute, it was obvious she was talking to her editor. She wrote training manuals for different companies—guess someone has to. Knowing the call could last forever, I made my way upstairs.

The new *Teen Vogue* was lying on Jilly's desk. I grabbed it, took it to my room, and threw myself across my bed. I hung over the side, staring down at my matted pink and purple shag carpet. When I was nine, my parents let me redo my room, with Barbie pink walls and *this* carpet. I just *had* to have it. What was I thinking? My eyes ran along the baseboard, looking for a ripple or bubble, something big enough to get my fingers under. I was tempted to start ripping it up that very second, put my frustration to good use. Probably an all-day job, though. Maybe I'd save it for tomorrow. Or maybe I'd get Dad to do it on the weekend. He'd be way better at it than I would. I flipped open the magazine.

"You're back early," Mom said.

I looked up, surprised she was off the phone. She seemed a little frazzled and had at least three pencils sticking out of the hair piled on top of her head.

"Yeah." I returned to the magazine.

I felt the mattress shift as she sat down on the corner of my bed. "Something happen? You two are getting along okay, aren't you?"

I didn't answer. I just kept turning pages but a little more violently.

"Was Sam there?" she prodded. "I know Jilly asked him to a movie, but if you have a crush on him too…"

"Mom! Stop!" Sputtering and choking, I rolled over onto my side. "Why would you say something like that?! I *totally* do not have a crush on him!"

She held up her hands in defense. "Whoa, sorry I brought it up. I just thought I picked up on a little something."

"What are you talking about?" I grumbled. "And FYI, nobody says *crush* anymore." I was starting to feel a little lightheaded over the fact that apparently the whole world knew I had a crush on Sam.

"It's okay, he's absolutely adorable. And tall," she added. "All the boys in your group are so short."

"Mom! I don't *like* him! And in case you didn't know, Jilly called first dibs." It sounded even stupider when I said it out loud.

"You see him more than she does," Mom pointed out. "And you know Jilly, she'll have her eye on someone else before the week is over. She goes through boys like they're on a Rolodex."

"A what?"

"Never mind. Before your time."

"Let it go, Mom. I'll just stay out of Jilly's way, thank you very much. Do you want to find me in a shallow grave in the backyard?"

"*Fine*. Like I said, sorry I brought it up." She sighed and got up to leave.

I pulled at a loose thread on my bedspread. There was a tug of war going on inside me. I took a deep breath. "Mom?"

She turned in the doorway.

"What do you think of Mrs. Swicker?"

"Well…I'll admit, she's a bit unusual."

"What would you say if I told you I think she killed her husband?" I just threw it out there, then braced for her reaction.

She did a double take, like something from a cartoon. "Pardon me?"

I repeated my question but softer, basically because Mom was looking a little scary, like she was going to snap any second.

"Lydia, is this some kind of *test*?"

"Mom. You've gotta check out this woman. She's hiding something, I know it. She has these dreams. 'I had to do it. You made me.' That's what she yells. And no one knows what happened to Sam and Megan's father. It's like he's fallen off the face of the earth."

Mom didn't respond. But she looked even more scary, if that was possible. Making matters worse, Jilly appeared in the doorway.

"You know, Lid…"

"Get out!" I shouted.

She ignored me and flopped across the bed beside me. She slid the magazine over in front of her. *Typical.*

"She could be talking about *anyone* in her dream," Jilly continued.

"How long have you been in the hall listening? Mom! Make her get out!"

"She could be dreaming about a friend or something, or if it *is* her husband, it doesn't have to be something *that* awful. Like maybe she spent all his money, you know, left him penniless." Jilly was on a roll. "And like maybe he deserved it."

"I think if it's causing nightmares and she's yelling, it's probably a little worse than that." I wanted to add "you idiot," but I knew better.

"Well, I couldn't imagine anything worse than that," she

stated, scratching and sniffing a perfume sample.

"Oh my God! Mom! Please make her leave!"

"Jilly," Mom sighed. "Could you please leave, I want to talk to Lydia *alone*."

Crap. "It's okay, Jilly, you can stay."

"Nice try." She flashed me a triumphant grin, and scurried out of the room. Of course she took the magazine with her. I could still smell the perfume sample.

"Lydia, I honestly don't know what I'm going to do with you." Mom sat back down on my bed. "Where in the world do you come up with these ideas?"

I sat up. "There's something wrong with Mrs. Swicker. I really mean it, Mom. What about the barbecue? She wouldn't come, just like I said! And I never told you about our trip to the waterfront. When we—"

"Just because someone doesn't want to come to our barbecue, doesn't mean they're a murderer." She cut me off. "And you better not be sharing these wild ideas with Sam and Megan. God knows what could get back to Mrs. Swicker."

I bit my lip. I was fighting a losing battle.

"How would you feel if someone made the same accusations about me?" she added.

"But Mom, you don't act like you're crazy!" *Most of the time.*

"Lydia. Allow me to make this perfectly clear. I don't want to hear anymore talk like this, not a word. Do you understand me?"

She was actually wagging her finger at me, like I was a

five-year-old.

"Fine!" I said it kind of nasty, through clenched teeth.

"Would you like to rephrase that?" Mom asked, folding her arms.

I was defeated. The only person who would suffer would be me. "Fine. Not another word." I beamed a fake smile, zipped my lip, and threw the imaginary key over my shoulder. "Guess I was just being overly dramatic. Must be all those wacky teenage hormones and stuff." I made my voice sound super chipper.

She looked at me suspiciously. "Yeah, must be." She closed my door softly behind her.

I picked up my pink, heart-shaped pillow with the sequins, and tossed it across the room. It was just all so unfair. My ditzy sister was trying to get her claws into my future husband, plus, I was pretty sure I was living across the street from a murderer, and of course no one believed me. I threw myself back on the bed and pulled a pillow over my face. Could my life get any suckier? I didn't know it yet, but apparently it could.

chapter

It was inevitable. The date had been rescheduled. I'd been
so wrapped up with my new theory, the box of baby stuff,
renewing my efforts to get back in that furnace room, not to
mention being worried that I'd majorly ticked off Megan, that
I momentarily forgot about Jilly's efforts to scoop Sam.

She was making toast when I went to the kitchen for some
breakfast.

"I've got a date with Sam," Jilly sang. She turned, waiting
to see if I'd say anything. She could be such a witch.

I gave her a sarcastic thumbs-up, refusing to comment or
ask for any details.

"And you said his mom wouldn't let him," she added smugly.

The urge to scratch her eyes out was overwhelming. I
walked out of the kitchen and back to my room without a
word, without my breakfast.

I didn't want to be around for the pre-date preparations,
and I certainly didn't want to be around for the post-date

debriefing. Was it possible I could just leave town for a few days?

The doorbell rang.

"Lid!" Jilly yelled. "It's for you!"

Megan was standing in the doorway. "Hi," she said, as I came down the stairs.

I was surprised to see her. "What's up?" I looked past her shoulder to see if Mrs. Swicker was hiding in the bushes or something.

"I was wondering if you wanted to catch a movie tonight."

"Ummm…you're not mad at me?"

She smiled and shook her head. "No."

"Because I'm really sorry. Sometimes I just say stuff without thinking."

"It's fine. I was…tired, that's all."

"Right," I nodded. "The not sleeping thing."

"So a movie?"

"Sure."

"Just so you know…Mom's taking us. She'll pay, though. A thank you for looking after Peter."

I could tell by the look on Megan's face that she was expecting me to change my mind. But what was the point of that? It wasn't like I had anything better to do. Plus the thought of being here when Sam picked up Jilly… "That would be great," I said.

Megan breathed a sigh of relief. She was about to leave, then spun around. "Oh yeah, Mom wanted me to get my key back."

My lying gene immediately kicked in. "Ooooh...I had Jilly's hoodie on when I fed Peter and I put the key in the pocket, then Jilly wore it to Vivian's and left it there. I'll get it back right away though."

A look of panic flashed across Megan's face. "Okay...Just get it as soon as you can."

I nodded, chewing the inside of my lip. I didn't want Megan to get in trouble, but there was no way I was ready to part with that key yet.

"What time are we leaving?" I asked, changing the subject.

"About ten after seven."

"See ya then."

• • •

The van was idling loudly in the driveway when I crossed the street to meet up with Megan. It was as though Mrs. Swicker's impatience was being blown out through the exhaust pipe. I checked my watch—it was exactly 7:10. I took a deep breath and slid open the door.

It's funny the way things work out sometimes. If anyone had suggested I might experience a moment of joy during this movie outing, I would have called them a liar. How wrong I would have been. When I opened that van door, imagine my surprise when I saw Jilly and Sam crammed into the back seat. My mouth hung open, my eyes bugged out of my head.

"Hey, Lydia," Sam said as though nothing was unusual.

I wanted to say hey back, but no words came out. I hopped up into the seat beside Megan. Mrs. Swicker peeled away from the curb before I even had the door closed. I stared straight ahead, pinching my lips together, trying not to smile. The look on Jilly's face was seared onto my brain, a combination of horrified and mortified with a touch of excruciating pain thrown in. Too bad there wasn't some magical way I could make it into my screen saver.

Megan was watching me the whole time. I could feel her eyes on me. Somehow I had a feeling she knew exactly what I was thinking.

Leaning over I whispered, "You could have told me it was a group outing."

"I thought you might not want to come," she whispered back.

"I wouldn't miss this for the world."

The drive to the theatre was...odd. Jilly and I never spoke or acknowledged each other's presence. I was dying to turn around and give her some kind of look, but I didn't want Sam to see. Mrs. Swicker didn't utter a sound, not that I expected her to. Sam and Megan chattered away as if this was all so normal, but it *so* wasn't. Every few minutes I just wanted to break out into fits of maniacal laughter. There was something about this whole situation that I found hysterically funny. Guess Megan wasn't the only one who was overtired.

Once inside the theatre, Mrs. Swicker actually let Sam and Jilly break ranks and sit by themselves. Unfortunately we weren't so lucky. She waited to see where they sat, then ushered Megan and I into seats a few rows back. The house lights were still on, so I wasn't worried about Sam and Jilly, *yet*. I glanced over periodically as Megan and I made small talk. I couldn't think of too much to say, and Mrs. Swicker was listening to every word anyway. Megan told me how Sam had just received an invitation to play a solo at the conservatory.

That caught my attention. "That's great. When's that again?"

"Thursday night."

Day after tomorrow. I filed that information away for later.

The movie was some romantic comedy. I didn't pay much attention. My view of Sam and Jilly was pretty good. They were about four rows in front of me, diagonally. My eyes adjusted to the dark and zeroed in on them. Their heads constantly touched because Jilly wouldn't stop whispering in his ear. I've been to movies with Jilly, she never shuts up. After about thirty minutes, my eye muscles were so tired from looking sideways, I had to stop. Digging my fingers into my eye sockets, I massaged my eyeballs.

"Are you okay?" Megan whispered.

"Yeah, yeah, I'm fine."

I focused my eyes again on Sam and Jilly, hoping I hadn't missed anything. I was waiting for the classic yawn and stretch. If it actually happened, I wasn't sure how I was going to react. I had a vision of me jumping up and screaming "Nooooo!" across the dark theatre. Mentally I glued my butt to my seat. I didn't have to wait long. It was beautifully executed. Jilly was truly a master. Sam probably didn't even notice that all of a sudden her arm was now around his shoulder.

"Hey! Watch it, would ya?"

Apparently I had squeezed my popcorn bag in a kind of reflex action and managed to empty half of it onto the lap of the girl sitting beside me.

"Oh, sorry." I felt like a total idiot.

By the time the movie was over, I was worried I had done permanent damage to my eyes. I couldn't stop blinking. We quietly filed out of our row and met up with Sam and Jilly in the lobby. Jilly seemed royally miffed or something. I was pretty sure nothing resembling making out went on between them. I don't think they ended up doing *anything*. Poor Jilly. I was starting to change my mind about not wanting to hear the post-date debriefing. But I bet she wasn't going to be so eager to share the details of this one—probably not one of her success stories.

The whole way home, I noticed Mrs. Swicker's eyes hardly ever left the rear-view mirror. She was trying to monitor Sam and Jilly, who were sitting together in the back seat, and of course now it was dark, making it harder for her to spy. When she almost drove us off the road, I finally let loose my pent-up hysterical laughter. Everyone in the van looked at me as though I was a raving lunatic.

If Jilly had some scenario in her head of a romantic goodbye neck fest under the porch light, she was sooo out of luck. Mrs. Swicker barely let them say see ya before she marched Sam and Megan up the driveway. Once again, Jilly and I were left standing there, just watching them.

Jilly followed me to my room and collapsed onto my bed. "Ohmygod, was that the most brutal evening of your life or what?" She had her arm flung over her eyes. "By the time I realized what was happening, that the Swickster was actually coming, it was too late to do anything."

"It wasn't that bad, was it?" I wasn't sure if I should agree with her or not.

She rolled over and sat up on her elbows. "Oh come on! That woman *honestly* needs help."

"At least she didn't sit with you."

"She might as well have. I could feel her eyes drilling into the back of my head the whole time."

No, that was me. I nodded sympathetically.

"Anyways," she continued. "It's never going to work."

"What? Why?"

"God, all he talked about was his violin and music. Mozart this, Beethoven that. Like seriously, shoot me now. All I know about Beethoven is from that movie with the dog...yeah, I have to end it."

"Um, Jilly, you've been to one movie, and that was with his mother. Is there really anything to end?"

"Look, Lydia, I've been down this road enough times, with enough guys to know it only takes one date, and they fall head over heels. I just have this magnetisism or something."

"Magnetism," I corrected.

"What?"

"Nothing."

"Back to what I was saying," she sighed. "I'm nipping this in the bud right away."

"Well, you tried, Jilly. If he's not for you, he's not for you. I mean you gave him a good three hours of your life. What more can you do?"

"I know," she said sadly. "I'm never getting those three hours back, either."

I sat down beside her and rubbed her back in the most comforting way I could muster, the whole time thinking that sometimes things just work out.

chapter

15

"Holy crap! What's that smell?" I squished up my nose as I entered the kitchen.

Jilly was standing in front of the oven looking puzzled. "I dunno. Mom left us this frozen pizza for supper. I followed the directions."

Smoke began to fill the inside of the oven. I hip-checked her out of the way and whipped open the oven door. "Jilly! You're supposed to take it off the cardboard!" I grabbed an oven mitt and a flipper and pulled out the smoking pizza, tossing it on the stovetop. "God, Jilly, next time just leave the plastic wrapper on so we can laminate the damn thing!" I fanned the air with the oven mitt.

"It didn't say anything about the cardboard!" she said, grabbing the box and scanning the directions.

"Look," I pointed, "*Place pizza directly on rack!*"

"Still doesn't say anything about the cardboard! You know, that's kind of like false advertising or something. It's obviously not as easy as they make it seem on the box!"

I seriously didn't know if I was going to be able to hang in another year until my parents shipped her off to some university. Halifax is a university town, and I lived in constant fear that she'd want to go to one here and, you guessed it, live at home. I'd gotten into the habit of dropping little tidbits of information here and there, like, "You know, Jilly, Mount Allison" (three hours away) "was voted best party university." Or, "I think Mom would be so touched if you went to Acadia," (an hour away) "it being her alma mater and all that."

I heard a clunk as Jilly frisbee'd the empty box across the kitchen and it hit a chair.

"Well, what are we going to do now?" she whined.

I peeled the pizza off the cardboard. The crust was totally raw. "I'll try putting it on the lowest rack, maybe the crust will catch up to the top." I slid the pizza back into the oven and pulled my butt up onto the counter. I looked out the window, across the street to the Swickers' house. I squinted, looking for signs of movement.

Jilly was watching me. "You better knock it off. Mom's really ticked at you. I heard her talking to Dad. They're thinking about sending you away to boarding school."

"What?!"

"Okay, they're not, but still…I'd watch it if I were you."

I gave Jilly a dirty look, but she was right. For all I knew, I was on double secret probation at this very moment. Mom loved springing that one on us when we least expected it. It was so secret it wasn't even *on* the punishment pyramid.

Jilly opened the oven to check the progress of the pizza. "This is totally gross. I'm *not* eating this."

I rolled my eyes and continued watching the Swickers'. I wanted so badly to get back into their basement, to go through that box again. I couldn't stop thinking about it. Megan hadn't asked for the key again. I just needed to hold onto it till tomorrow. Tomorrow was Thursday, Sam's thing at the conservatory. But I didn't want to go in alone. I needed a lookout.

"I'm ordering out!" Jilly slammed the phone book on the table. *But who?*

"If you want some of my pizza, you're paying for half!" *I need someone I can trust.*

"I mean it. Go get your wallet. I want the money up front!" *Someone who's smart.*

"You know, it's so weird that there's no T in pizza. No one says peeza or pieza, everyone says peetza."

I swung my head to look at Jilly. She was still flipping through the phone book. *I need someone besides her.*

"Quit staring at me and go get some cash," she ordered.

I slid off the counter and headed to my room. The hamster in my head was going a mile a minute, round and round on his wheel. There was no way it could work. The number of things that could go wrong with Jilly as my accomplice was endless. If only Vicki and William weren't at their cottages…

but they were. I really had no other choice. The upside was, at least Jilly agreed with me that Mrs. Swicker was a nut job.

I looked around my room for my wallet. I dug through a few drawers. Success. I grabbed a five and a toonie and jammed them in my pocket.

As I walked back to the kitchen, I wondered if I could maybe blackmail Jilly into helping me. Racking my brains, I searched for anything I had seen or heard that I could hold over her, but there wasn't anything. She was nearing the end of Phase Two, and counting the days until she was able to move onto probation. She knew she'd better not step one toe out of line.

I handed her my money. How much I could trust her? How desperate was I?

We both sat at the table and waited for the pizza. Jilly was scraping the mascara off her eyelashes. I couldn't seem to take my eyes off her. Using her thumb and finger, she methodically moved down her lash line, stopping to look at the black on her fingers before flicking the claylike crust onto the floor. It was fascinating in a disturbing kind of way.

"Oh! Get this!" she exclaimed. "I broke it off with Sam this morning. I swear he looked at me like I had four heads or something!"

"Yeah…probably just didn't see it coming." I could only imagine what he must have been thinking. It was *one* movie. With his *mother*!

"Damn." Jilly stared at her fingers, a giant frown on her

face. "I pulled a bunch out! Didn't I read somewhere that eyelashes take forever to grow back in?"

"I doubt it." Of course I was referring to the implication that she had actually read something. I didn't have a clue how long it took eyelashes to grow in.

"Yeah, didn't think so."

I began carrying on a whole conversation in my head. Jilly? Or no Jilly? Weighing the pros and cons.

She was watching me with a weird look on her face. I'd probably been moving my lips.

"Are you having some kind of spell or something?"

I couldn't believe I was about to do this. "Jilly, I think I might need your help."

The doorbell rang. The pizza was here.

"Hold that thought," she said.

Maybe that was a sign. It wasn't too late. I could make something up, like I wanted her to highlight my hair or give me a pedicure.

Jilly put the box on the table and opened the lid. She poked the pizza. "It's still pretty hot." She looked up. "So what do you need my help with?"

That kind of threw me off. She actually seemed interested. "Well." I paused to swallow, my throat felt dry all of a sudden. "If you really want to know, I want to sneak into the Swickers', when they're not home, obviously, and I need someone to come with me, someone to be a lookout."

"Sure." She slid a piece of pizza onto a plate.

"What?"

"I said sure."

"Don't you even want to know why?"

"No."

Now this was an unexpected surprise. "What, no 'What's in it for me?' or 'How much is it worth to ya?'?"

"No," she said, as she flicked her finger and broke the foot-long string of cheese that stretched from the slice to her mouth.

This was way too easy. "I don't get it."

"Nothing to get," she stated. "I know you think Mrs. Swicker is some crazed, psychotic, killing machine. I actually believe at least two out of those three adverbs."

"You mean adjectives."

"Whatever."

"But you took Mom's side when I told her."

"Well *yeah*. I know you don't think I'm the *sharpest* pencil in the drawer, but I'm not the *dumbest* either."

I bit my lip to stop myself from smiling.

"Plus," she continued. "You can't expect me to take your side while Mom's jumping down your throat, that just puts me in more trouble than I am already. I want that extra hour back on my curfew in this lifetime."

"If we get caught, though, you're toast. We both are."

"Pfft, we're not gonna get caught." She waved a hand in the air. "This is going to be totally awesome. I've always wanted to do something like this, you know, break in under the cover of darkness and all that."

"I got a key."

"Dark clothing, surveillance, hiding in bushes...wait. You got a key?"

"From when I fed Peter."

"Oh." She seemed a little less enthusiastic now that we weren't *physically* breaking and entering.

"Come on, Jilly, don't you want to hear my plan?" I had to reel her back in.

"Okay, lay it on me."

"All right. They're not going to be home tomorrow night. Sam's playing a solo. Megan will go too because Mrs. Swicker won't leave her home alone. It's at the conservatory, so that's a good twenty minutes travel time both ways, plus the actual performance. We should have loads of time—a quick in-out." I picked a piece of pizza up from out of the box and bit off the end.

"So what are we looking for? A knife? A gun? Weapons of some sort?"

I almost choked on a wad of cheese. "No, nothing like that." I grabbed a napkin and wiped my mouth. "There's a box in the furnace room. Inside are two silver rattles. I have to get a better look at them, see what else is in there. I ran out of time before."

She gave me a look like she thought I was crazy. "You think she beat her husband to death with a couple of rattles?"

I sighed heavily. "No, Jilly."

"Well what in the world could a couple rattles have to do with anything?"

"I dunno." I got up and poured two glasses of milk. "That's what I'm hoping to find out. I can't get rid of this feeling that she's hiding something."

"Hmmm," Jilly rubbed her chin, deep in thought (or wiping off tomato sauce). "Okay, I'm in. And by the way, you owe me another loonie for half the pizza guy's tip."

chapter

The Swickers' van pulled away at seven o'clock. We'd have at least an hour and a half. I went to look for Jilly, even though I had told her about twenty times to be ready *before* seven.

She was in her room filing her nails, her hair wrapped up in a towel, turban style.

It felt like my head was going to explode. "Jilly! I told you to be ready! What's the matter with you?!"

"Chillax, would ya? I'll be ready in two secs." She bit her lip. "I don't suppose I have time to dry my hair, do I?"

"Uh, *no*…you don't." My blood was boiling.

Jilly got ready surprisingly fast, finishing off with a dab of lip gloss.

We stood on our front step, looking up and down the street. I wished it was later, darker.

"Where's Mom and Dad?" Jilly asked.

"They went to Sears to look at lawn mowers."

"Oh." She looked down and pointed to the envelope in my hand. "What's that?"

"I thought of this at the last minute. If someone sees us going up to their house, we could say we're returning a letter that was delivered to our house by mistake." I held it up so she could see it had the Swickers' address on it. There was even a stamp.

She looked impressed and nodded her head.

We tried so hard to look nonchalant and casual as we crossed the street, but our body language was screaming "Guilty!" I was so nervous, tiny giggles kept erupting from my body.

My heart was pounding loudly in my ears as we stood at the Swickers' front door. I pulled the key from my pocket. The bell on the end of the key chain tinkled, sounding like cymbals crashing. Why is it when you try to be super quiet, every little noise seems extra loud? Peter appeared, purring at our feet.

"Hurry up," Jilly whispered urgently.

I got the door open and she pushed me inside. We each took a deep breath and I wiped my sweaty hands on my shorts.

"Okay," I said. "You stay here and watch the street. I'm going downstairs."

"Oh no you don't. I'm coming too."

"Jilly! That was the deal! You're the lookout, remember?"

"Uh-uh, there's no way I'm going to be the one standing here if Mrs. Swicker walks in the front door. I'm coming with you."

"Apparently I should have held some kind of seminar to explain the role of lookout," I hissed.

"Just stop talking. You're wasting time."

I sighed. She was right. We could always fight about this later. "Come on then."

We hurried downstairs. I led the way to the furnace room and flicked on the light.

Jilly nudged me. "Check it out." She was pointing to a box with a bunch of vodka bottles. All empty. "Someone has issues."

I nodded my head. But that wasn't the box I was interested in right then.

"There it is." I lifted it down off the pile. It seemed to be the way I'd left it.

Handing the pink blanket to Jilly, I told her to unroll it. I lifted out the blue one and felt for the rattle inside. We both pulled them out at the same time.

"*Amy Elizabeth*," Jilly whispered. "What's yours say?" She leaned over.

Her long wet hair draped across my face. "Give me some room!" I pushed her back. The heat in the furnace room, the stress, and the smell of Jilly's strawberry shampoo was making me feel sick to my stomach. I held up the rattle and read the engraving. "*Michael Edward*."

Jilly and I looked at each other, the same confused expression on our faces. We held both rattles out in front of us, side by side.

Same rattle, same style of engraving.

"Look," I pointed. "Same date. *July 1, 1994.*"

Jilly turned to me. "Twins!"

"Who *are* these kids?" I frantically dug around in the bottom of the box to see if there was anything else that could be a clue. A couple soothers, a tube of diaper cream, and a flattened, quilted diaper bag. I lifted up the diaper bag to check underneath. It felt kind of heavy. I unzipped the zipper and stuck my hand in and felt around. "I think there might be something else…" My voice trailed off as my brain registered what I'd found. Even though it was wrapped in a blanket, there was no doubt what I'd grabbed onto.

Jilly took one look at me. Her eyes widened. "What? What is it?"

I pulled it out. I peeled back the baby blanket. A gun.

Jilly shot to her feet. "I asked if we were looking for a gun! You said no!"

"Well I didn't know it was here, now did I?"

"Just put it back, put it back, put it back," Jilly frantically whispered.

"I am, I am." But for a second I just stared at it. I'd never seen one close up. Even against the blanket of cartoon yellow duckies—it totally scared me. It scared me more to think it might be loaded.

There was a loud noise. My entire body jerked and my stomach dropped like an elevator.

"Just the furnace," Jilly breathed.

My eyes darted to the huge metal contraption clunking away in the corner. "Let's get out of here," I said. With shaking hands, I quickly wrapped the gun and put it back in the bag.

"Yeah, I'm starting to get freaked out."

My legs were wobbly when I stood up. Jilly helped re-roll the rattles and I placed the box back on top of the pile.

I took a final glance around the furnace room, turned out the light, did the same thing upstairs, and locked the front door. Jilly and I forced ourselves to walk at a normal pace back to our house. Once inside, we bolted up to my room. Jilly closed the door firmly behind us.

"We're okay. Mom and Dad are still out," I said, sitting down at my desk and resting my head in my hands.

Jilly sat down on the corner of my bed. She was breathing deeply, trying to calm herself down.

The thoughts in my head were whipping around like a windstorm. Amy and Michael. Who were they? *Where* were they? And the gun? What about the *gun?*

Jilly must have been thinking the same thing. "You know… people are allowed to own guns," she said, almost like she was reasoning with herself.

"Yeah, I know."

"Like, she *is* a single woman, living alone."

Jilly was right. Someone in Mrs. Swicker's situation might think they needed a gun, but, "If she had it for protection, wouldn't it be in her bedside table, or in a kitchen canister or something? Somewhere she could get to it quickly? Not hidden in a diaper bag in the basement."

"Yeah...you're right." Jilly looked stressed.

The gun thing was kind of stressing me out too. Then I had a thought. "I suppose we could be way off. Maybe at one time she had a gun for some reason, like they lived in a bad neighbourhood or something, and now she's packed it away because she doesn't feel she needs it anymore." I wasn't sure if I believed that, but it *was* possible, and it definitely lowered the scariness level.

Jilly looked thoughtful, but didn't agree or disagree. "So who do you think these kids are then?" she asked.

I shook my head slowly.

"I guess all we know is that they're twins," she said.

"They'd be about my age..." My birthday was June twenty-third.

"And about Megan's age," Jilly pointed out. "Maybe she has another brother and sister, besides Sam, I mean."

"Her age? No, that doesn't make any sense."

"Maybe she's a triplet."

"No...I can't imagine that's it. And where are they, then?"

Jilly looked at me with raised eyebrows. "You're the one who thinks Mrs. Swicker's capable of murder. And now you have a weapon."

"Yeah, but I'm thinking worst-case scenario she did something to her husband, not her kids. Even I don't think she's capable of *that*. And Megan would have told me if she had another brother and sister." I started to doubt myself. "At least I *think* she would have…" I drummed my fingers impatiently on the desk.

"Well, who could they be?"

I stared back at her blankly. I was as puzzled as she was.

The sound of car doors slamming drifted in through the window.

"Mom and Dad are back," Jilly announced.

"Girls!" Dad called up the stairs. "Come see the new lawn mower!"

Jilly rolled her eyes. "Oh *joy*."

We trudged down the stairs and out to the front lawn.

"Check it out, girls," Dad said, both arms pointing at the shiny new lawn mower, his new baby. "Is she *sweet* or what?"

"She's beautiful, Dad," I said.

"We shall call her *Gabrielle*," Dad sighed.

I looked at Jilly.

"She's so high-tech, she'll practically mow the lawn herself," Dad cooed, caressing the handle bar. "You girls could do it in no time flat."

Jilly made a choking noise. "Can we be done looking at the lawn mower now?" she asked loudly.

"Sure, girls. Thanks for showing some interest."

Jilly tugged on the sleeve of my T-shirt. "Come on."

I was just closing my bedroom door when Mom's arm sliced through the opening like something out of a slasher flick. She pushed open the door, came in, and sat on the corner of my desk.

"Okay, girls, spill. What are you two up to?" Her eyes were narrowed and her tone oozed with suspicion.

"What are you talking about?" Jilly asked, sounding totally innocent.

"Call me crazy, but the last time you two willingly spent time together behind closed doors was in the late nineties."

"Mom, you're overreacting," I said.

"Well…it's just a little out of character, wouldn't you say?" she asked.

"Mom. We're just talking. You should be encouraging us, not *frying* us." Jilly crossed her arms.

"Maybe you're right," she nodded, not looking convinced. "Maybe I'm overreacting." She started to leave, then stopped and turned. "I *hope* I'm overreacting."

Once the door closed, we both let out a huge sigh.

"Maybe we should just tell Mom and Dad what we found," I suggested.

"Oh, okay, brainiac, love to see you work *that* into a

conversation. Especially the whole breaking in part. Plus," she put her face really close to mine, "there's no way you're taking me down with you. If they shave any more time off my curfew, my life is over."

"Technically, we didn't break in," I said, but I knew she was right.

"Look. Obviously us hanging out together in plain sight is causing a ripple in the universe or something, so I say we break for tonight, sleep on it, meet up tomorrow when Mom's busy with other things."

"Okay," I nodded. "Tomorrow we'll figure out where we go from here. Assuming you want to keep trying to find out who Amy and Michael are."

"Well *yeah*."

"Okay then, that's what we'll do."

chapter

"Hmmm…what to do, what to do…" Jilly lay on my bed, thinking out loud.

I watched her pick up my pink sequined pillow, toss it up in the air, then catch it. She did it over and over.

Something instinctively told us not to ask or involve Sam and Megan. The fact that we *both* felt this way we took as a sign. We decided that if we were going to find out who Amy and Michael were, we had to get as much info on Mrs. Swicker as possible—she was the key.

After making a list of all the strange things we'd observed or discovered concerning Mrs. Swicker, we rated each item on a weirdness scale of one to ten. Everything came in at a nine or better. The whole waterfront slash gift-shop incident actually rated an eleven, tied with the box in the furnace room.

"God! I wish I had been in that gift shop with you!" Jilly groaned.

I cringed inside as a tiny wave of guilt washed over me, knowing I had strategically planned it so she *couldn't* be in that gift shop. "Yeah, me too."

"Give me the instant replay, one more time."

"Jilly, I already told you everything I remember."

"And that lady seemed sure Mrs. Swicker was this Reenie Barretto?"

"She seemed pretty sure to me."

"Well, do you think you can remember her name?" Jilly asked.

"I don't see how that's going to help us."

"Maybe we could track her down, talk to her."

I burst out laughing. "Are you nuts? How are we going to do that? Not to mention, we can't just call up a complete stranger!"

"She could be our last resort, you know, if we can't find anything on our own. Just try to remember."

I closed my eyes and pressed my fingers against my temples. I could feel Jilly staring at me, waiting for me to say something.

I went through the scene step by step. The woman with the sunburn pouncing on Mrs. Swicker, me behind the cookbook rack, Mrs. Swicker turning pale as a ghost, the woman poking herself in the chest, saying, "It's me, Phyllis…*something*, of course now I'm Phyllis…*something else*…smoking Kools under the bleachers…it's me, Phyllis…"

"Gregory!" I shouted. "She said her name was Phyllis Gregory!"

"Excellent!"

I shook my head. "But that was her name in high school. Let me see if I can remember her married name." I lay down beside Jilly on my bed and tried to focus. I began to go through the alphabet in my mind, trying to remember the second name she'd said. "Of course now I'm Phyllis...*Phyllis A..., Phyllis B..., Phyllis C...*" It's what I always did when I was trying to remember a word, especially a name.

"What are you muttering?" Jilly asked.

"Shush!" *Phyllis L...Phyllis M...*I sat up. "Phyllis Mmm..., Phyllis Maaa..., Phyllis Mooo...Munroe! Her name's Phyllis Munroe!"

"Now we're getting somewhere!" Jilly got up and began pacing the floor, rubbing her hands together.

I rolled over, resting my head on an elbow and watched her, wondering if perhaps some kind of alien had taken over her body.

She noticed me looking at her. "What?"

"No offence, Jilly, but I guess I'm kind of surprised how into this you are. You really seem to want to help."

She frowned and took her time answering. "Well...I guess I sort of see it as a whole new experience. I don't think you've ever asked me to help you with anything before."

I opened my mouth to argue but then closed it. Maybe I hadn't.

"Okay, enough of the heart-to-heart. Get me a pen and paper and let's get some of these names down," Jilly instructed. The non-alien one. Only the *real* Jilly would consider two sentences a heart-to-heart.

Grabbing a piece of loose-leaf and a pen from my desk drawer, I jotted down *Phyllis Munroe,* then added *Phyllis Gregory,* just in case. I didn't need to check for the other name, *Reenie Barretto.* It had stuck in my head from the moment I'd heard it, like some annoying commercial jingle.

After much deliberation, we decided we needed Mom's computer. The computer downstairs was the first and obvious choice, but it was Saturday, so Dad was home, and he always made a point of checking over our shoulders whenever we were on the computer. Mom was at Costco, or the Hundred Dollar Club, as Dad liked to call it. "Can't seem to get out of there for under a hundred bucks," he always said. We figured Mom would be gone for at least two hours.

"I checked on him," Jilly said. "He's watching a cooking show. Let's hit Mom's office."

I nodded and followed Jilly down the hall. Our steps slowed as we got closer to the office door. To be honest, Mom didn't really ask that much of us. There was *one* thing that she was pretty firm about, though, and that was that everyone stayed out of her office and no one touched her computer, not without some kind of written request. Usually the only time our fingers were allowed to land on those keys was when Jilly and I had assignments due at the same time, ones that required use of the internet. Even then, Mom remained in the office, terrified we were going to mess up her stuff or delete something by accident.

"God. If only Dad would break down and get wireless, then we could just use my laptop," Jilly grumbled.

"Good luck with that." Dad didn't want us to be able to be online anywhere out of his peripheral vision.

"Make room," Jilly demanded, as we both squeezed into Mom's leather chair.

"Who do you want to do first?" I asked.

"Pick a name…any name."

"Let's Google Reenie Barretto and see what comes up," I suggested.

Jilly typed in the name and we held our breath.

"Wow, not much here. It's kind of a weird name…nothing that looks like what we're looking for anyways."

"Try Facebook."

Jilly clicked on and typed in the name again. A picture of a pretty woman with long hair, cuddling a newborn baby came up on the screen. "So not her," Jilly said.

"What about Bernadette Swicker? Try that."

"On Facebook? No way Mrs. Swicker's the Facebooky

type—commenting on photos, updating her status, posting pictures—I just don't see that happening…" But Jilly tried it anyways. A bunch of names came up, slightly off in the spelling. None of them were her.

"Go back to Google," I said.

Jilly typed it in and we waited. She scrolled down one page after another, and another, and another. "And here I thought nobody would spell Swicker with an S. Oh wait. Here's publishing credits for her photography." Jilly clicked the mouse. "Doesn't say anything about her, though."

"Maybe you were right," I admitted. "Maybe we should try to find Phyllis. Go back to Facebook."

"Yes, Master," Jilly sighed and put in the name.

"That's her!" I pointed to the picture. It was the woman from the gift shop. Different floppy hat, but definitely her. I scanned the screen. "She must have high privacy, no info about her. We could send her a message, though."

"Let 'er rip." Jilly had her fingers poised over the keyboard.

"Just put 'Reenie Barretto wants to say hi.'"

Jilly sent the message. "But now what? Who knows when she'll check her email. She's probably not like us. We're on the computer all the time, check our email twenty times a day. She's like…old."

"She could even still be on that cruise." I fiddled with the corner of the mouse pad and thought really hard. "Maybe we *should* try for her phone number. Go to 411.com, and type in Phyllis Munroe."

Jilly did as I asked. "It wants a state," she said.

"Crap. Let's go by alphabetical order, I guess. Alabama?"

We both leaned in close and studied the page. I was amazed that sometimes it even gave their ages. It helped eliminate some names. I jotted down a couple possibles as we went through each state. This was taking way too long. We were still on the C's and Mom wasn't going to stay at Costco forever.

As I stood up to stretch my back, I had a thought. I remembered that the cruise ship was a Carnival cruise out of Miami—someone had mentioned it in the gift shop. "What are the odds that if the ship sailed from Florida, some of the passengers might *be* from Florida?"

"I dunno, it's worth a shot." She typed in FLA.

It practically jumped off the page. "There! Phyllis and Jerry Munroe, 2262 South Atlantic Boulevard, New Smyrna Beach."

We sat there, our eyes darting back and forth between the phone number on the screen and the phone.

"This is insane! We can't do this! What are we going to say?" My voice kept getting higher and higher. "Why are we doing this again?"

"Think about it. Aren't you dying to find out if Reenie Barretto *is* Mrs. Swicker? I mean, this Phyllis person might know all about her, or at least be able to give us a clue." Jilly looked at me intently. "I mean, what if you're right? What if she *did* murder her husband? And where are those other kids?"

I chewed on my lip.

"This is way faster than waiting for Facebook," she pointed out.

"We have to figure out what to say."

"Well...the truth is out."

I chewed harder. "You know, with the right spin, the truth could be a possibility. Like if we say we're worried about the kids."

"Huh...that's just crazy enough to work. I'll dial."

Phyllis answered on the third ring. I took a deep breath and, speaking clearly and calmly, told her who I was and began my story about our new neighbours. I explained how I had been in the gift shop that day and saw everything that went down between the two of them. That the woman she thought was Reenie Barretto we knew as Bernadette Swicker. I could tell she was under the impression she was talking to another adult and there didn't seem to be any point in correcting her. I went on to tell her how I had observed some strange behaviour from Mrs. Swicker, and fudged a little when I kind of *implied* that her children might be being mistreated. I kept waiting for her to cut me off, hang up, but she didn't. She wasn't standoffish or anything, she actually seemed quite intrigued by the whole thing.

"We're just so worried about the children," I added.

"I understand completely. If she's pretending to be someone else, you've got to wonder why. Surely there's a reason," Phyllis said.

I asked her if she was still sure that Mrs. Swicker was the girl she went to high school with.

"I don't know if I'd stake my life on it, but I'm fairly certain. She still looks exactly the same." Phyllis paused. "She was such an odd bird, not easy to get to know. Always skulking around with that camera of hers, snapping pictures when you least expected it."

I swallowed hard. "Mrs. Swicker is a photographer."

"Now that's quite the coincidence, isn't it?"

"Do you have a picture of Reenie Barretto you could send us?"

"Ummm...her yearbook picture, maybe."

"That would be great. And possibly anything else you can remember about her."

"I'll have to sit down and think about that for a bit, but if anything comes to me I'll send it along. You have a fax number?"

I gave it to her and thanked her. She made me promise to keep her posted.

Jilly sucked in her breath. "There's Mom's car. Abort! Abort!"

I hung up the phone. "Shut down the computer. We have to make sure everything's the way it was."

Jilly took a final frantic look around and practically shoved me out the door. We tore down the hall back to my room. We were lounging casually on my bed when Mom stopped in the doorway. She was flipping through a pile of mail.

"There're some boxes in the trunk of the car," she said without looking up. "Can you girls bring them in for me?" She continued down the hall to her office.

We hadn't even made it to the stairs.

"Jilly!" It was Mom.

We looked at each other.

"If you're going to be sneaking around where you're not supposed to, you might want to think about changing to an unscented shampoo! It smells like a fruit farm in here. And what's this paper with the names on it?"

"You left the paper?" I gasped.

"Never mind that now. She's coming. You're a way better liar than I am. Think of something."

I didn't know whether to be flattered or offended. "Tell her they've been linked to Robert Pattinson or something," I whispered just as Mom came around the corner.

"Sorry, Mom, I was just Googling some names," Jilly said.

I couldn't believe she was taking the fall all on her own.

"They're just names of girls linked to Robert Pattinson," she explained. "I wanted to get the scoop, you know, check out the competition."

Mom raised her eyebrows. "And what was wrong with the computer downstairs?"

"Lydia was on MSN Messenger. I asked her about twenty times to let me have a turn, but she wouldn't."

My mouth dropped open. I should have known.

"Hardly an emergency, Jilly," Mom sighed. "Please don't make me ban you girls from the computer. And I don't want to have to start locking my office door, either. You know how I feel about people mucking around in there."

"Sorry. It won't happen again." Jilly was the picture of remorse.

Mom took another look at the piece of paper before handing it back to Jilly. "Phyllis Munroe. Isn't she in that new movie with Julia Roberts?"

"Hey, I think you're right, Mom," Jilly said, nodding.

Mom returned to her office and closed her door.

We both rolled our eyes and shrugged.

chapter

It's amazing how your brain keeps working, processing, even when you're asleep. *Damn!* My eyes flew open and I sat bolt upright in my bed. The numbers on my clock radio glowed 2:08 in an eerie blue light. I threw back my covers and padded down the hallway to Jilly's room.

She lay on her back, hair curled up in Velcro rollers, purple furry sleep mask covering her eyes.

I poked her on the arm. "Jilly," I whispered.

Nothing.

"Jilly!" I poked harder.

She moaned and rubbed her arm. Lifting up a corner of her mask, she glared at me with one eye. "What?"

"We screwed up," I said. "We told Phyllis to fax us the stuff, but we didn't tell her when. Mom's going to find it, or *hear* it. You know the racket that thing makes."

"Shit!" Jilly whipped off her mask and sprang out of bed. "Well, we have to call her back, give her a specific time or something."

"One...it's quarter after two in the morning, and two... how are we going to explain that? Our *mom* only lets us receive faxes during certain times of the day? Phyllis thinks she's dealing with a grown-up, remember?"

"Damn you and your...your...super-mature voice."

"She probably wouldn't have been so keen to help if she thought I was just some punk kid," I defended.

"I guess." She crawled back into her bed. "Let me think for a sec...Wait, I think I got it."

"Okay, give it to me."

"Vivian."

I didn't need to hear any more. "Uh-uh, no way."

"Cool your jets. Her dad's got a fax machine. We'll just tell Phyllis that ours isn't working and have her fax the info to Viv's number."

"No, no, no," I said, shaking my head. "You know she'll want to know every single detail."

"No she won't," Jilly argued. "She couldn't care less what we're up to."

"Yeah right. What planet are *you* on?"

"Okay, then." She folded her arms. "We'll go with your idea."

I gave her a dirty look and sighed. "*Fine.*"

Back in my own bed, I fought to keep my eyes closed, determined to get some sleep. The thought of staring at the clock, waiting for the next five hours to pass, was starting to stress me out. It didn't feel like it, but I must have dozed off at some point because the next time I looked at my clock it read 7:58.

I lay in bed, formulating a game plan. I'd have to wait until ten o'clock our time to call Phyllis, that would make it nine in Florida. Mom usually spent a couple hours in her office after breakfast. That would be a good time to make the call. Then there was Vivian. Maybe I'd just let Jilly handle her. Vivian was way too hard on my head.

First, I got Jilly to call Vivian to get her fax number.

"Didn't she want to know why?" I asked.

"No. I told you, she couldn't care less, she just said 'Sure, whatever.' She probably won't even look at the fax. She was planning on highlighting her hair, you know, the one where you pull the hair through the cap? It's *very* intense. It'll keep her busy for the whole day."

"She'll let us know when it comes?"

"Yup. She'll send me a text."

Next I called Phyllis. She told me she'd dug out the yearbook stuff and that she'd fax it to the new number sometime today. I wanted to press her for an exact time but I didn't want to push my luck.

The day felt excruciatingly long. Jilly and I stuck together, hanging out in the family room watching TV. Mom kept looking at us with her eyebrows scrunched together, but we just smiled back. Finally, at 4:12, the muffled melody of

Hedley's latest song could be heard—Jilly's ring tone. She flipped open her phone and read the text. "She wants us to call," she said, dialing Vivian's number.

I pressed my head next to hers and she tilted the phone so I could hear too.

"So…I got your fax," Vivian said. There was something in her tone I didn't like. "There's a picture here," she continued. "And I'm pretty sure it's your crazy neighbour, Mrs. Swicker."

"Ummm…" Jilly stalled.

"You guys better get your butts over here," Vivian bossed. "And I want *Every. Single. Detail.*"

I pinched a piece of flesh on Jilly's arm and twisted as hard as I could.

chapter

"Where are you guys off to?" Mom asked suspiciously. She found us practically tripping over each other to get out the door.

Jilly and I looked at each other. "Uhhhh...Vivian's having a hair crisis. She's highlighting her hair and she can't reach the back. Mom, we gotta go. You know it's all about the timing," Jilly explained.

"And why are you going, Lydia? This doesn't seem like your kind of thing."

"Uhhhh...I'm thinking about trying one of those kits out before school starts. Just wanna see how it turns out." I was talking way too fast.

"Hmph."

I could tell she didn't believe us, but what could she say?

We were just about to make a break for it when everything went in the crapper. Who was strutting up our front walk? Mrs. Swicker, and she didn't look happy.

"Lydia!" she snapped.

My feet froze to the spot.

"I've just been made aware of the fact that you are still in possession of Megan's house key." She pretty much spit the words at me.

"Oh right, ummm, let me get that for you, sorry about that."

"I'll wait for you outside, Lid, okay?" Jilly squeezed past Mrs. Swicker, who was blocking the front door as though she thought we were going to flee the country with her stupid key.

"It's in my room, totally slipped my mind," I lied. Tearing upstairs, I grabbed the key, desperate to get rid of her. Not that I thought she'd hang around for a friendly chat or anything like that, I was just dying to get to Vivian's.

She snatched the key from my hand, spun around, and left without a word. Even Mom looked a little flabbergasted.

"Lid! Hair! Timing!" Jilly was jumping up and down on the front step.

Mom stopped me again. "That reminds me, take your key. Your father and I will probably be gone by the time you guys get back."

"Where are you going?"

"Dinner, a show, then overnight at the Hilton. It's our anniversary, remember?"

"Oh, I totally forgot." I felt bad. I didn't even get them a card. "Have a great time. I'll make it up to you, promise." I stood on my tiptoes and kissed her cheek.

"I'll hold you to that. Now don't forget, Jilly's babysitting tonight around the corner. You could go with her if you don't want to be alone, and I'll leave the number of the hotel by the phone."

"Mom, don't worry, I'll be fine."

Jilly and I were out of breath by the time Vivian's house came into view. Vivian stood on her front step, her brilliantly platinum hair beckoning to us like a lighthouse.

"Wow, nice hair." I couldn't help myself.

She shoved me into the door frame, hard.

"Ouch!"

"Yeah, well I got a little distracted by *your* junk, and I left the stuff in too long. I want the scoop," she demanded, waving a finger back and forth between me and Jilly. "You guys *so* owe me."

I started to break out in a nervous rash just thinking about how long it was going to take to tell Vivian the whole story, let alone make her actually *understand* it.

Jilly must have picked up on my body language. "I'll fill in Vivian, you start going through the stuff from Phyllis." She turned to Vivian. "Is it in your dad's study?"

Vivian nodded. "Down the hall on the left."

"Wait. Are your parents here?" I asked.

"Nope. Golfing."

Surprisingly, the study *was* down the hall on the left.
For some reason I expected her directions to be wrong.
There were a few sheets of paper sitting beside the fax
machine. The copy of the yearbook photo was on top.
I let out a little yelp. There was no mistake, it was Mrs.
Swicker. Plunking myself into the leather office chair,
I hungrily devoured the information in my hands. The
name under Mrs. Swicker's photo read Noreen Baratto.
No wonder we couldn't find anything, we were looking
for Reenie Barretto—not even close. I quickly read the
yearbook write-up: *Noreen, aka Reenie, can usually be
found snapping pictures for the yearbook committee. She's off
to the big apple next year to attend Tisch School of Arts for a
degree in Photography. Reenie leaves Coral High with these
words, "Get away from me!" We wish her well.*

My mouth dropped open. I had to laugh. Now *that* was
funny. Had she known they would put that quote in the
yearbook? She probably didn't care one way or the other.

Vivian and Jilly tumbled into the study.

"What's so funny?" Jilly asked.

"Here, read this." I handed her the piece of paper. Vivian
read over Jilly's shoulder.

"Well, if the picture didn't convince me that this is Mrs.
Swicker, the write-up definitely did," Jilly smirked.

Vivian sat on the corner of the desk. "It's just so out there,
you know? Like, do you really think she's on the run? That she

did something to Sam and Megan's father?"

I sighed. "I don't know. It's just a theory. I don't have any proof."

"And these other kids, the twins, are they *her* kids? Where do they fit in?" Vivian asked.

"At this point, we're hoping whatever we find out about Mrs. Swicker will help us figure out who they are," Jilly said.

"Well, she changed her name. She must be hiding from *something*," Vivian pointed out. "Seems to me the something *has* to be the father. He's the bad guy, and she's protecting the kids from *him*. Did you ever think of that?" Vivian asked.

Megan had suggested that, but, "No." I shook my head. "No, I never did."

"Trust me," Jilly said. "There's no way that Mrs. Swicker's gonna turn out to be the good guy, no way."

"You never know…" Vivian sang.

"Well, we do." Jilly dragged a footstool over next to my chair. "What else you got there, Lid?"

I pulled out another piece of paper from under the yearbook page. "She wrote down some stuff and there's a photocopy of a newspaper clipping."

"Read it!" They demanded in stereo.

"Okay, um…her note says…*Forgot I cut out this wedding announcement, found it stuck in my yearbook. It might help. I do know I read in some newspaper column, they were divorced in less than a year.* Here's the article," I continued. "*Kennedy-Baratto.*

*Announcing the upcoming nuptials of John Kennedy of Phoenix,
Arizona, and Noreen Baratto of Miami, Florida. The couple
will marry in a civil service on September 23, 1991. The bride
elect is the daughter of Gladys and Murray Baratto of Miami,
Florida. The future bridegroom is the son of Eleanor and Carson
Kennedy of Phoenix, Arizona. The bride elect has just obtained
her degree from the Tisch School of Arts. The future bridegroom
is a recent graduate of Juilliard School of Music, and has accepted
the prestigious position as conductor of the New York Symphony
Orchestra."*

I rested the papers on my lap and leaned back in the chair,
digesting the information.

"Okay," Jilly said. "This John Kennedy must be Sam and
Megan's father."

"Well, we have to find out if he's still alive," Vivian said.
"Like to rule out if Mrs. Swicker did him in, right?"

She was right, which kind of threw me. I spun the chair
around to face the computer. Clicking onto Google, I typed
in John Kennedy. We waited. The screen popped up with lists
of websites, a bijillion to be exact. "*Duh...*" I sighed. "John
Kennedy, as in *John F. Kennedy*, the president. Same name!
We'll be here for hours!"

We sat there staring at the screen. John F. Kennedy
biography, John F. Kennedy memoirs, John F. Kennedy
assassination, it went on forever.

"It'll probably be the same on Facebook," Vivian said.

"Stay on Google. Type in New York Symphony," Jilly suggested.

I perked up and typed it in.

"Oooh…pictures!" Vivian clapped her hands together.

"Look! There he is, John Kennedy, conductor. *He's alive!*" Jilly exclaimed.

"And look what else. There's a slideshow of news and upcoming events. Maybe we can get a better picture of him, even some info," I said, clicking the mouse. "Here we go… says he's the youngest conductor blah, blah, blah…casts a spell with his baton blah, blah, blah…and here's a good picture… looks about the right age to be Sam and Megan's father."

"Doesn't look half bad in a tux either," Vivian pointed out.

"Yeah, tuxes really are the most amazing things. They can make even the most loserly guys look hot. Not that this guy's a loser," Jilly added.

I rolled my eyes. "Can we focus, please?"

Jilly flicked the back of my head with her finger. "Just put up some more pictures."

We scanned through the photos, the different performances, guest musicians, mumbling to ourselves as we frantically read the blurbs, waiting for something to jump out at us.

"Stop!" Jilly shouted. "Click on that one. He's got his arm around a woman."

"Okay…um…seems pretty recent…the date says April 30,

2009…looks like some kind of party, let's see what it says…"

Jilly cut me off. "National Center for Missing and Exploited Children?"

"Hey! Stop reading ahead!" I snapped. Taking a deep breath, I read out loud from the column under the picture. *John Kennedy and wife of sixteen years, Samara Nolan-Kennedy, mingle with guests after performance benefiting the National Center for Missing and Exploited Children. This is the thirteenth performance of its kind organized by the Kennedys. All proceeds are donated to the National Center for Missing and Exploited Children."*

"So Samara's his second wife…" Jilly said.

Vivian and I slowly nodded our heads.

"And they're big into this missing kids centre because…his kids from his *first* marriage are missing? Sam and Megan?" Jilly continued.

"I guess…" It made sense, but something didn't feel right. It just wasn't coming together in my head. I reached over for the wedding announcement from Phyllis to check the dates. "John Kennnedy and Mrs. Swicker, or *Baratto*, married in 1991." I thought about that for a minute.

"And remember, he didn't stay married to Mrs. Swicker for very long," Vivian said. "Less than a year."

"Have you *met* her?" Jilly asked.

Vivian smiled. "Probably felt it was time for an upgrade."

"Guys, listen, think about it." I flipped over Phyllis's fax and began drawing a timeline on the back. "If Swicker and Kennedy married in '91, but divorced in less than a year…" I scribbled the events and dates on the line. "Megan's my age, born 1994, Sam's just over a year and a half older…" I made more marks on my line. "It's off. The dates don't fit."

A look passed over Jilly's face. I knew she was experiencing a light bulb moment. She leaned in really close to the screen. "Lid, can you make that picture bigger? To get a better look at wife number two?"

"Think so." I clicked a couple times.

We all sucked in our breath at the same time.

"What the…?" Vivian's voice sounded far away.

"She looks just like Megan," Jilly whispered.

My eyes were popping out of my head. It was Megan, but it wasn't. It was Samara Nolan-Kennedy, but there was no doubt in my mind. *She* was Megan's mother.

chapter

I whipped the chair around. "Megan's not her kid!"

Jilly had figured it out, but Vivian wasn't there yet.

"Mrs. Swicker, she's not Megan's mom. It's totally obvious from the picture," I explained to her.

"But Sam...he's older...could *he* be Mrs. Swicker's?" Jilly asked.

Frowning, I picked up my timeline and stared at it. "I suppose she could have been pregnant or something when they divorced. It *could* fit...maybe?"

"What about the twins, though?" Vivian cut in. "They're still floating around out there."

"I know." Things seemed to be getting more complicated by the minute. I turned back to the computer. "There's got to be a connection somewhere." Jilly and Vivian huddled around me and we stared at the photo. "I can't believe how much she looks like Megan." I made a circle around Samara Kennedy's face with the cursor.

"Wait! Stop!" Vivian's silver-blue fingernail tapped on the screen. "Right there! A link!"

Sweeping the cursor back over the photo, a blue bubble popped up. *Learn more about the Kennedys' story.*

"Click it!" They both shrieked right into my ears. The page seemed to take forever to load. There was something happening in the room, a kind of electricity or excitement that kept growing every time I clicked the mouse.

A website popped up. "*The Kennedy Kidnappings?!*"

"Oh. My. God!" Jilly's mouth hung open. "Look at the website address—kennedytwins.com."

"*Twins*," I whispered

"Read it!" Jilly screamed.

I began to read at lightning speed.

"Out loud!" Vivian smacked the back of the chair.

"Sorry, sorry." I cleared my throat, licked my lips, and began. "*Introduction. This site is dedicated to the disappearance of Amy and Michael Kennedy. There are few residents of Long Island who have not heard of the Kennedy Twins or have forgotten the tragedy of that day in 1995.*" Jilly and Vivian were so close I could feel them breathing on my neck. It was stressing me out. I motioned with my hands for them to back off, then continued. "There's a couple baby pictures and a link to that missing kids centre. Okay, it goes on…*Case in Brief—On August 29, 1995, Emily Bradford, the Kennedys' nanny, placed the one-year-old twins in their playpen on the back*

patio of their home on Long Island. She then went inside to do
some housekeeping while they slept. When Ms. Bradford went back
to check on the twins, the playpen was empty. She called the police
immediately.

During the investigation many tips poured in, but none that
led to an arrest. The Kennedys hired private investigator Romeo
Tucci, a retired FBI agent, to aid in the search. Mr. Tucci was
quoted as saying 'It's a very unusual case, no ransom note, no paper
trail, no forensic evidence left at the crime scene. We seem to run
into one dead end after another.'

A psychic investigation suggested the twins were taken by a white-
collar ring of businessmen who used infants in ritualistic sacrifices.
This theory was dismissed by both the Kennedys and the police.

No trace of the infants has ever been found. Although the police
have named several suspects over the years, no one has ever been
charged with their abduction.

John and Samara Kennedy live a quiet life, still in the same
house where they lived with their children. They never give up
hope that someday they will be reunited.

This case remains unsolved to this day."

The room was perfectly still. No sound, no movement, no
air. My mouth felt completely dry, like I'd been walking for
days in the desert.

"Megan is Amy," I finally said.

Jilly stared at me intensely. "And Sam is…"

I nodded my head slowly. "Michael. He has to be." That

had to be the answer. In a bizarre way, it was the only thing that made sense.

"What?!" Vivian cried. "No way! Sam can't be her twin, they're not even the same age!" she added.

"Just think about it for a second." I tried to keep my tone calm. "There's no reason why they *couldn't* be twins. They *could* be the same age."

"Ewwww," Jilly cried.

"What?"

Jilly began to frantically wipe her tongue on the sleeve of her T-shirt.

"What are you doing?!" I yelled.

"I kissed him!" She made a gagging sound like she was trying to cough something up.

I momentarily forgot everything that was going on around me. "What?" I whispered. I could practically hear my heart breaking in two.

"Oh, it was quick, thank *God*. Outside the van."

"So what's the big deal?" I asked, devastated.

Jilly looked at me as though I was covered in open sores. "It means he's…" She stopped to sniff. "Your age!"

My mouth dropped open. "That's what you're freaking about? Get a grip, would ya?!"

Vivian swooped to the rescue. "It's okay, Jilly, your secret's safe with me," she soothed, rubbing Jilly's back. "I'll take it to my grave, I swear."

"Could we get back to what's important here?" I tried not to sound too sarcastic. "Do we all agree Sam and Megan *could* be twins...*could* be the mystery twins?"

Jilly sniffed again, smoothed her hair, and pulled herself together. "I suppose," she answered reluctantly.

Vivian thought about it for a minute, twisting a piece of platinum hair around her finger. "Yeah...yeah, I guess so."

"I suppose Mrs. Swicker could have just *told* everybody that Sam's older. People would believe her. *We* did," Jilly said, a pained expression flashing across her face. "I bet she thought it would be easier to keep them hidden if she passed them off as regular brother and sister. Everyone was looking for twins."

"Exactly." I was sort of impressed by Jilly's reasoning. "And she'd changed her own name, of course she would change theirs too."

We fell quiet again, thinking, organizing our thoughts.

Vivian broke the silence. "So, just so I've got this straight, Mrs. Swicker gets the boot from famous husband. Famous husband remarries, has twins. Mrs. Swicker kidnaps twins for what? Revenge? Is that what you guys think?"

"Kind of sounds like something she'd do," I said. "There might be more to it, but yeah, that's pretty much what I'm thinking." Then something occurred to me. "You know, Sam and Megan don't even know they're twins."

"Whoa, now that just totally blows my mind." Vivian had now wound that piece of hair so tightly around her finger I could see the tip starting to turn blue. "This is like *way* too intense. Are you sure you're right about all this?" She looked like she was about to hyperventilate.

"Just *relax*, Vivian." I wanted to slap her, like they do in the movies when someone gets hysterical. The situation probably wasn't that extreme, but I still wanted to try it. I didn't, though. Turning to Jilly, I said, "I think we should print off all of the information we found."

"Yeah. That way we have proof in our hands when we go to…the police?" She sounded unsure.

I nodded my head. "I think maybe we should tell Mom and Dad first."

"You're probably right."

Jilly and I retraced our steps on the computer and printed off all the information we thought was important. Except for the sound of the printer, and Vivian doing some kind of deep breathing exercise to calm her nerves, it was eerily quiet. It was as though the excitement had evaporated when we realized the seriousness of the situation. When we were done, I put Phyllis's faxes on top, straightened the pile, and paper-clipped the corner. I stared at Mrs. Swicker's, a.k.a. Noreen Baratto's, yearbook picture. "Fourteen years, and she's never been caught," I whispered.

"You don't think we're wrong, do you?" Jilly asked, like maybe she was having second thoughts.

"No. Do you?"

She paused for a second. "No."

We left Vivian lying on the couch, a damp facecloth draped over her eyes and forehead.

The Swickers' house came into view as we turned the corner. My steps slowed.

"Come on." Jilly pulled me firmly by the arm. "We can't do anything about it this minute."

"I know, I know, I just want so badly to tell them…now." My voice caught in my throat. For some reason I felt like breaking down and crying right in the middle of the street.

"It's going to be okay," Jilly said. She put her arm around my shoulder. It was so out of character it made me flinch. It dawned on me that she was trying to be comforting.

"But they have no idea they have real parents out there, parents who love them, parents who probably think they're *dead* or something." I could feel my lip tremble.

"I know," she said quietly. "But we're not the ones to tell them."

I turned and took a long look at Jilly. It was kind of freaking me out how calm and logical Jilly was being about everything. I'd always thought of myself as the adult in our relationship, the fixer of things, the level-headed one. It was as though we'd had a total role reversal.

I rattled our front doorknob in frustration. "Locked!" Then I remembered. "Mom and Dad aren't here!" I cried. "It's their anniversary." I leaned my forehead against the door.

"Damn. That's right." Jilly glanced at her watch. "And I'm supposed to babysit in like two minutes."

I dug the key out of my pocket and unlocked the front door. "I really wish Mom and Dad were here."

"We'll call them right now and tell them what's going on," Jilly said.

My eyes kept darting out the window, across the street. "Call Mom first."

Jilly dialed. My heart fell as my ears picked up a faint ringing from upstairs. Without a word I walked past Jilly, upstairs to our parents' room, and picked up Mom's cellphone off the bureau. I flipped it open. "It's me."

"Put Mom on," Jilly demanded.

I shook my head and snapped the phone closed. Jilly was still shouting "Hello? Hello?" as I walked back into the kitchen. She looked at me and said, "Oh," as I waved Mom's phone in front of her face.

"Try Dad," I suggested.

She punched in the numbers, then screwed up her face. "It went right to voicemail. I'll leave a message."

"Mom mentioned a show, they're probably at Neptune. I bet he's got it turned off." I slumped onto the kitchen chair. "The number for the hotel should be beside the phone. Leave a message at the front desk too."

Jilly found Mom's note and called the hotel. She left a message for them to call home when they got in.

"Maybe we should just call the police now, or that missing kids place," I said.

"No!" Jilly looked horrified. "You can't do that without *me*. Don't worry, Mom or Dad will call back soon, we'll tell them everything, they'll know what to do." She checked her watch again. "Crap! I'm supposed to be at the Robertsons'."

"Go. You're gonna be late."

She stopped at the front door. "I think you should come with."

I flashed back to the last time I babysat Noah and Angus Robertson. It was five months ago and I was still having nightmares. "Nah." I shook my head. "My head's pounding. I just want to lie down."

Jilly looked torn. "Okay. You know the Robertsons' number if you need me. Oh, and there's a couple DVDs on my desk that I forgot to return. Crawl in bed and watch a movie or something, maybe it'll take your mind off things till the 'rents call. And phone me right away when they do."

"I will, and don't worry." I pushed her out the door. "I'll be fine."

chapter

Scream 3, The Grudge, and *When a Stranger Calls.* Those
were the DVDs Jilly suggested I watch to help take my
mind off things. I left them on her desk and padded down the
hall to my room.

There it was, perched on the top shelf of my bookcase, my
most prized possession: *Titanic, 3 Disc Special Collector's Set.*
I lifted the case down and ran my fingers lovingly over the
fabric cover—my version of comfort food.

Even though it was a hot August night, there seemed to be
a weird kind of chill in the house. I wrapped myself tightly in
my Hello Kitty blanket.

Passing the phone on the hall table, I stopped and stared at
it really hard hoping my telekinetic powers would kick in and
make it ring, make Mom call. I had an upset feeling in the
pit of my stomach. Uneasiness, or *nerves,* whatever it was, I
wanted my mom.

Truthfully, there was still a teeny part of me that hoped
we were wrong about Mrs. Swicker. It would be way easier
knowing you lived across the street from some freakazoid

nutcase, instead of a real live criminal. There was *some* reassurance in the fact that if we were right, and this all hit the fan, she would be history. But Megan and Sam would probably be gone too. What was going to happen to them? Especially when they found out Mrs. Swicker wasn't their mother? How was it all going to go down? I could feel myself getting more anxious by the minute, so I tried to block out those thoughts for now.

In the family room, I popped the DVD into the player and curled up on the sofa. My eyes filled with tears before the mournful notes of the theme song finished. It got me every time. The excitement and stress of the past few days was catching up with me. Weariness seemed to be seeping into every inch of my body. The last thing I remembered were the words "This ship can't sink!"

When my eyes flew open, the room was in total darkness except for the flickering light from the TV screen. It cast creepy moving shadows along the wall. I pressed my hand to my chest. It felt as though my heart was going to jump right through my skin.

A half-frozen Kate Winslet was floating, hanging onto a deck chair, blowing a whistle over and over again. Sighing with relief, I realized it had probably just been the sound of the whistle that woke me. I wiped some stray drool from the corner of my mouth and squinted at my watch to check the time. 10:21. Why hadn't Mom and Dad called?

A noise echoed through the darkness. It sounded like a doorknob slowly turning.

"Jilly?"

No answer.

"Jilly?!" I called a little louder.

Again, no answer. But then there was a strange shuffling sound.

There was a pounding in my ears as all the blood in my body drained to my feet. My hand darted out to the lamp but at the last second I snatched it back, afraid to turn it on. I didn't call Jilly's name again. Something told me it wasn't her.

But someone was in the house.

Slowly I rose from the sofa and inched my way through the dark towards the kitchen, hoping to quietly slip out the back door. I must have been holding my breath. I felt dizzy and had to keep grabbing onto pieces of furniture for balance.

I was one step away from the kitchen. About to cross the threshold, the light flicked on, making me freeze like a statue. It took a second for my eyes to adjust.

There she was, leaning against the wall. Mrs. Swicker, her hand still on the light switch.

I jumped, startled. What could she possibly be doing here? I was totally confused.

"Hello, Lydia," she said coolly.

I was still trying to clear my head and didn't reply.

"You know, Lydia," she began, then stopped to root around

in the giant purse that hung messenger-style across her body. "Here we've been neighbours all this time…" She pulled out a giant bottle of vodka, slowly unscrewed the cap, and tossed it on the counter. "And we've never really gotten to know each other."

My eyes grew wide.

"So let's do that." She took a swig from the bottle. "Let's get to know each other."

She came towards me. I noticed the bottle was already half empty. I shrank back against the doorframe.

With her foot she slid a chair out from under the table. "Sit down, Lydia."

My brain was sending me a message to be afraid, to get out. Quickly, my eyes darted around the kitchen and I shook my head no. Sitting down would place me farther from the door, from a way out.

Her eyes narrowed at my defiance. "How did I somehow know you weren't going to make this easy?" She took another mouthful of vodka.

I tried to make a break for the door, but she was surprisingly fast and side-stepped, cutting me off. "Oh no you don't!" She gestured with the bottle for me to get back, spilling some on the floor.

This was nuts. *She* was nuts. I was terrified.

"What are you doing here?" I finally worked up enough courage to ask.

"Oh…I think you can probably figure it out."

"I—I don't have a clue." But it was slowly dawning on me. *She knows. She knows I know. Why else would she be here?*

"Cut the crap. I know you're lying." Her voice was icy as she hissed the words through clenched teeth.

I could feel myself break out in a clammy sweat and goosebumps both at the same time. "No I'm not," I whispered.

"Do you really think I'm that stupid? That I don't know a *liar* when I see one?"

"Honestly, Mrs. Swicker, I don't know what you're talking about." I continued to deny her accusations. Then, trying to sound calm and confident, I said, "I'm expecting Mom and Dad home any second, you know."

"Lydia, Lydia," she said, shaking her head. "Don't you think I've thought of that? I've been on a stakeout all day. You know what a stakeout is, don't you, Lydia?" she asked in a sly tone, but didn't wait for an answer. "I saw your parents leave earlier with a suitcase, and I also saw that bimbo of a sister of yours traipsing up to the Robertsons'. I know she's babysitting."

I was going to argue, but I couldn't make my voice work.

"I knew you were trouble the minute you opened that yappy trap of yours," she continued, a crazed look in her eyes. "The incessant questions. How many times I just wanted to slap your face and scream at you to *shut up!*"

There was a huge lump in my throat that I couldn't swallow, no matter how many times I tried.

With an unsteady hand, she raised the bottle to her mouth.

I heard the glass hitting her teeth. It made me shudder.

"And now I have to—" Her next word was covered by the sound of the bottle being slammed down on the counter.

"Have to w-what?" I stammered, even though I was afraid of her answer.

"*Move!*" she screamed. "I have to *move! Again!*"

Tears were beginning to collect in the rims of my eyes. No Mom and Dad, no Jilly, no help. I was on my own. It was like being trapped in one of Jilly's movies.

"I swear, I—"

"Stop!" she screeched. "Not another word. I'm not going to let you screw it all up now. I've worked too hard, too long. Not you. Not some smart-ass kid who thinks she's the next Nancy Drew."

"I won't, though. I won't screw it up! I don't even know what you're talking about!"

She ignored my words and just looked at me like I was the most despicable thing she'd ever seen in her life. "You're more clever than I thought, I will give you that much. It took me a while to figure it all out."

"Figure out what?" My instincts told me I would be safer if I kept her talking.

"That you knew my secret, of course."

I opened my mouth, but she cut me off. "Don't bother denying it. You're not as smart as you think you are. You left a trail."

"A trail?" I frantically searched my memory, trying to figure out what she meant.

"The night of the recital," she explained. "I watched Megan put that damn cat out before we left, but when we got home, *ta-dah!* There he was—inside."

I could feel my eyes widen. I remembered. I remembered the bell on Megan's key chain, how Peter showed up when we snuck in that night. He must have come into the house with us and we didn't notice.

"Of course I immediately went through the house to see if anything had been disturbed," Mrs. Swicker continued. "Nothing looked out of place, but then I remembered the box, that friggin' box! I checked it. *Someone* had been into it."

"Doesn't mean it was me," I insisted. "I wasn't anywhere near the furnace room."

"Who said anything about the furnace room?" she asked triumphantly.

My stomach dropped. "A guess?" I mumbled.

"Yeah *right*," she laughed.

I stared down at the floor feeling totally defeated. How could this not have occurred to me? It had never entered my mind that Mrs. Swicker would catch onto us before we had a chance to turn her in. It wasn't supposed to happen like this. We were going to be the heroes.

"Why didn't you just mind your own damn business?" she practically growled.

I wished I had an answer.

"But as it turned out…" She set down the vodka and smirked. "I had to get something out of the box anyway."

I watched her reach in her purse and pull out the gun.

chapter

I gasped out loud and pressed my back against the wall to keep from falling down. Fear churned in my stomach and spread out to the very tips of my fingers and toes. It was a tingling feeling, like I wasn't even in my own body.

Mrs. Swicker held the gun up to the light, lowered it, and polished a spot on the barrel with the hem of her shirt. "It was right there on the porch. The nanny had left it—yeah, that's right, they had a *nanny*. Couldn't bloody well be bothered to raise their own damn kids. I just grabbed it and threw it over my shoulder. Figured it might come in handy. Little did I know." She paused and sucked back some more vodka.

I finally clued in. The diaper bag.

"Didn't find them until later..." she continued.

I had to think for a minute. "The rattles?"

"Well, so much for 'It wasn't me, Mrs. Swicker, *honest,*'" she mimicked in a squeaky voice.

My lip was trembling so much I had to bite it to make it stop.

"My first instinct was to get rid of them," she admitted.

I shot a peek at the clock. Jilly might be coming home soon, maybe she would figure out something was wrong. Or Mom and Dad might get our message... *Just keep her talking.* "Why *didn't* you get rid of them? The rattles. Why did you keep them?"

She winked at me. "I came up with a plan."

"A plan?"

"Instead of just tossing them, I thought..." she tapped the gun against the side of her forehead, "no, wait. These could come in handy. What if... someday I needed money? Well, let me tell ya, that day's right around the corner. Actually, I'm surprised I've been able to go this long. The photography biz isn't what it used to be." She sighed wistfully and took another drink. "Fancy cameras cheap, all the things computers do now, people don't need a professional anymore."

She wasn't making any sense. "So you were going to sell the rattles?" I asked. Yes, they were silver, but how much did she think she'd get for them?

"No, you stupid girl!" Spit flew from her mouth as she yelled at me. "I could use them to extort money from their stinking father!"

Now I wished I had sat down when she told me to. My

knees had started to shake uncontrollably, but I kept going. "How? Use the rattles how?"

She seemed to calm right down, almost like she was happy to share her story. "All I'd have to do is get in touch, anonymously of course, demand money, *huge money* for their safe return. They'd want some proof I had them, and that's where the rattles come in. They're my proof—better than any photo. Like how are they to know what their kids look like now? But one look at those rattles and there'd be no doubt."

"And you'd give them back? Sam and Megan?"

She raised her eyebrows and shook her head. "Never." Then she smiled a giant evil smile. "Sometimes I considered sending the rattles by themselves, no note or anything, just to torture them."

I stared back at her, blinking in disbelief. How could someone do that? Be that awful? Explain it as if it were nothing, no big deal? It was like she wasn't human, like she was all black inside. I felt sweat trickle down my temple, along the front of my ear. I wanted to wipe it away but I was too scared to move.

"Don't you love Sam and Megan even a little?" I choked. "You loved their dad once."

"Sam and Meg are fine," she laughed. "They've never suffered. But oh, let me guess. You're trying to find my weakness, appeal to some ounce of decency you think I might have. Don't waste your time, honey."

"But you couldn't possibly want to do this…" I reasoned desperately.

The look on her face made me cringe. "You know *nothing* about me," she seethed, instantly enraged. "You may think you do, but you don't. I can't *stand* people like you." She pointed the gun at me, this time using both hands.

"Please. I won't tell, I swear I won't tell a soul. Just let me go," I pleaded.

Frowning, she relaxed her arms, acting calm again. "The funny thing is…" she said, wagging the gun like a finger, "I didn't even know how much you knew…but I thought I should play it safe anyway, just take the kids and run, pull a Houdini, that was the plan. I didn't, though. Want to know why?"

I nodded.

"Did a little test. Went to the computer, to Google, and typed in Amy and Michael, July 1, 1994. You'll never guess what popped up."

My mouth fell open. *Please, it couldn't have been that easy.*

She caught my expression. "That's *right*…kennedytwins. com! I knew you'd seen the rattles, the names, figured you probably tried the same thing. So it was official—you knew too much. I had to deal with you before I went *anywhere*."

I didn't answer. I was still recovering from the fact I hadn't been smart enough to think of that.

"Wait a second…" She squinted till her eyes were tiny black slits. "Who else have you told?"

"Everyone!" I shouted wildly. "Everyone knows! Jilly, Mom, Dad, the neighbours! I even called Nana Mary!"

"Hmmm…" She took another drink then proceeded to pick at the edge of the vodka label with the mouth of the gun.

She must have guessed I was bluffing because she didn't look very alarmed. I took another peek at the clock. It was almost eleven. "Why did you take them?" I asked. "Sam and Megan. Was it revenge? Spite?"

"Why?!" she shrieked. "Ah…because when my so-called *husband* became a *somebody*, he had an affair with some little skank, then left me for her. Someone younger, someone who could give him *children*! Good enough reason for ya?!" Her voice was dripping with disgust.

"I bet they'd forgive you, drop the charges if you gave them back. It's not too late."

"Give them back?!" There was an incredulous look on her face. "For fourteen years I've looked after these kids! I've fed them, clothed them, I've even *taught* them, for Christ's sake! I'm not giving them back, they're mine!"

"But they're *not* yours." Why was I arguing with her? How stupid was I?

"They should ha-ve been!" she hiccupped. "I read the papers, the society columns. The Kennedys, the *golden* couple, hosting their charity dinners, throwing fancy galas left, right, and centre! That was supposed to be me! My life! The big estate! The perfect children! The parties! It was all supposed to be *mine!*" She reached out to the counter to steady herself.

"How could they not know it was you?" I said it more to myself than her. I couldn't believe no one had figured it out.

Looking past me, she smiled. "My performance was Oscar-worthy. I was questioned and released, end of story." She continued to hiccup but stayed lost in the memory, like she'd forgotten I was there.

I wiped away some tears and weighed my options—I didn't really have any. Mrs. Swicker stood between me and the door. The phone was out of reach…but closer than the door. Was it possible to inch my way over? Didn't have a clue what I'd do if I got there. Would I have enough time to dial?

I took a step sideways into the kitchen. That was a mistake. The movement brought her full attention back to me.

"Don't move!" she snapped.

I just nodded and hugged my arms around myself to stop shaking.

She raised the bottle to her lips. Once again there was the sound of glass crashing against teeth. I noticed she had to tip it up really high this time.

I loudly sniffed back some tears, wiped my nose with the back of my hand, and began to cough like I was about to throw up, trying to distract from the fact that I was slowly moving another inch or so into the kitchen.

All of a sudden, Mrs. Swicker's eyes widened and darted to the window.

It was the sound of a car.

My heart leapt.

A car door slammed, then the sound continued down the street and faded away. I looked longingly at the door. In most horror movies, this would be the moment the boyfriend or best friend would burst in and come to the rescue.

No one came.

My heart sank.

They usually got massacred anyways.

Feeling as though all hope was lost, I asked, "Aren't you worried you'll get caught?"

"Of course I'm worried. I *live* worried. But I've learned to cope." Lifting the bottle level to her eye, she checked how much she had left, took a drink, then set it down. "You're but a speed bump on my road to the finish line. We'll be long gone by the time anyone figures anything out. I've become quite good at disapplearing." She gave her head a shake. "Disappearing."

With trembling arms, once again she aimed the gun. Her eyes blinked furiously as she tried to focus.

"Please…" I whimpered.

She did something that made a clicking sound, whatever it is you do before firing. I could feel my body shutting down, preparing for what was to come. My ears rang. More sweat dripped down my forehead into my eyes, making them sting. I could feel tears slide down my cheeks in a constant stream. I prayed I'd pass out and not feel anything. I prayed it'd be quick.

How much was it going to hurt? Would my parents come home and find me dead, surrounded by blood? Would they ever get over it?

I held my breath, closed my eyes, and waited for the bullet to rip through my skin. But it didn't come. I opened one eye.

She was staring at me, the gun clenched tightly in her hands.

"Hold still!" she screamed.

But I wasn't moving.

I let out a little cry and squeezed my eyes shut as tight as I could. And then something amazing happened.

The phone rang.

My eyes flew open. She still had the gun pointed at me, but instinct made her turn her head towards the ringing. In that second, I saw a chance. I spun around and grabbed a knife out of the knife block and lunged towards her.

Everything seemed to be in slow motion, though I knew it was over in a matter of seconds. Her startled look, the shock that spread slowly across her face as the knife made contact. And then the blood, everywhere the blood. Then…nothing.

The phone had stopped ringing. With shaking and bloodied hands, I picked it up and dialed 911, watching the red seep into the spaces around the rubber numbers. "Someone tried to kill me," I whispered. "But I stopped her…"

Between ragged sobs, I managed to answer the operator's questions as I slid down the wall to the floor and waited for the police. I don't remember much after that, like what I did while sitting there, or how long it took the police to show up. They were nice, though, I do remember that. They asked me if I was hurt.

"Toss me a blanket, Joe. I think the kid's in shock," one said. Another said they would try to track down my sister and parents. They helped me up and sat me in a chair. A paramedic came and gave me a checkup—I guess I passed. I watched in a daze as a never-ending parade of uniforms filed in and out of the house, taking pictures, sticking up bright yellow tape.

I sat at the kitchen table and stared at the blood. It formed a pool on the floor, surrounded by a kind of circular splatter design. It sort of reminded me of those paintings I did in preschool, the ones with the drops of paint squished between a folded piece of paper. There always seemed to be a big glob in the middle. The blood looked just like that. I wondered what I could use to clean it up. Mom gets hysterical about marks on the hardwood floors. She's probably going to freak when she sees this. She's going to freak about a lot of things.

The rotating light from the ambulance flickered through the kitchen and made it feel more like a disco than a crime scene. It bothered my eyes, so I moved my chair to face away from the window. I wanted to leave the kitchen altogether, but I didn't. Two officers stood a few feet away, talking quietly. They had just finished asking me some questions and had told me to stay put. I figured I was in enough trouble already—better not push my luck.

From my new angle, I could see the knife perfectly. It had spun, propeller-style, across the floor to rest in front of the fridge. Part of me felt compelled to pick it up before someone stepped on it, the other part of me knew better, knew it was now considered evidence. And I'd seen enough *CSI* to know they don't like it if you tamper with the evidence.

I couldn't believe things had gotten so out of hand. Things like this just didn't happen around here, not in this neighbourhood. At least they didn't before the Swickers moved in.

chapter

23

"Where is she?!"

It was Jilly's voice that snapped me out of my
trance. I'd been sitting at the kitchen table zombified for…five
minutes?…five hours? I looked up to see her shouldering her
way through a cluster of officers. One reached out to stop her
with his arm.

"I'm her sister!" she barked and shoved his arm away.

She looked absolutely terrified. "Are you okay?" she
whispered, kneeling beside my chair.

I nodded.

"Oh, thank God." She threw her arms around me.

As soon as she touched me, I dissolved into tears.

"Shhhh, everything's going to be fine." She put my head on
her shoulder. "Shhhh."

A female officer who had been sitting with me stood and
moved a few steps away to give us some privacy.

I wiped my nose on the sleeve of Jilly's shirt and leaned
back in the chair. I took a few shaky breaths and swept away

some pieces of hair that had caught on my wet eyelashes and in the corners of my mouth.

"What the hell happened?" Jilly asked, still whispering.

"Mrs. Swicker. She found out, found out we knew."

Her mouth fell open. "That's who's in the ambulance?"

"Yeah," I nodded. "She had a gun. I stabbed her." I said the words, but it didn't sound like my voice.

"She tried to *kill* you?!" Jilly exclaimed. "I heard the sirens, and saw the flashing lights. I thought it was a break-in or something."

"I wish..."

"What a friggin' psycho," she said softly. "And *she* could have been my mother-in-law..."

"I want Mom and Dad," I sniffed.

"The police told me they're on their w—"

"Lydia!" Mom screamed. She and Dad blew in like Hurricane Juan. Anyone standing around in the kitchen instantly parted and gave them a clear path. Mom grabbed me by my shoulders, looked me up and down, checking for damage I guess, then she crushed me against her body. A fresh supply of tears burst from my eyes. After a minute, she passed me to Dad and we repeated the process. Inspect, hug, cry. Wash, rinse, repeat—like the directions on a shampoo bottle.

"What? Happened? What was Mrs. Swicker doing in our house with a *gun*?" Mom tried to keep her voice calm by slowly enunciating each word.

I looked at Jilly and melted back onto the chair. I'd already told the police the whole story. I didn't have it in me to tell it again.

"I'll explain everything," Jilly offered.

She started talking but I couldn't follow what she was saying, it sounded muffled—far away and fuzzy. I saw that a bunch of officers had joined Mom and Dad to listen to her. I got up from my chair and pulled the blanket snug around me.

"You can't leave, Miss," a voice said. I turned. It was the officer from earlier, the one who seemed to be watching me.

"Please," I begged. "I just need to move around, get some fresh air."

She looked like she felt sorry for me. "I'll have to come with you."

I stepped outside just in time to see the ambulance pull away. The lights were flashing, but the siren was silent. I didn't know what that meant.

There was a white station wagon parked in front of the Swickers'. *Family Services* was written on the side. "Can I walk around a bit?" I asked.

She nodded.

I made my way a little further up the driveway, squeezing between two parked police cars.

A woman was standing on the Swickers' porch. Sam and Megan were with her. With one arm around each of their shoulders, she led them down the steps. They looked up and saw me. Even from across the street, I could see the shock, the fear on their faces. I darted out to the street to meet them, to see if they were okay.

"What have you *done*?!" Megan screeched.

I stopped in my tracks. Was she talking to me?

She broke away from the woman and marched toward me. "You tried to kill our mother!" She was sobbing but I could feel and hear her anger. "What's *wrong* with you?!"

"No! You don't get it. It wasn't me! It was *her*!" I cried.

Sam joined her. "We thought you were our friend," he accused.

I felt like I'd been punched in the stomach. "I *am* your friend! I was trying to help you!"

He put his arm around Megan. "We don't need your kind of help."

"Megan!" I reached out to grab her arm. I had to make them understand.

She looked repulsed and took a step back. "Get away from us! I don't want to ever see you again!" She yanked open the door of the station wagon and took a seat. Sam slid in beside her.

The woman gave me a sympathetic look. "You should just leave them for now, honey," she said.

I stood there stunned and watched them pull away. They didn't look back. There was someone standing behind me— the officer, but then I heard, "It's okay, I've got her. Could you just give us a minute?" It was Dad.

"Did you see them, Dad? Hear them? They hate me!" I said,

my voice quivering.

He pulled me back against him and rested his chin on my head. "It'll be okay, Pumpkin."

"I didn't think it would turn out like this…"

"You have to realize their whole world has been changed in an instant. Everything they thought they knew turned out to be…well, a lie."

"She had a gun. I *had* to do it. Dad…I was *so* scared."

"I know, I know," he soothed.

"And now they blame *me*!"

"Once they have the whole story they'll feel differently."

"You don't think they'll hate me anymore?"

"No, I don't think they'll hate you anymore."

"Are you just saying that?"

"No."

I wasn't sure I believed him.

"Come on. Let's go back in," he said.

The officer followed us inside to the living room and stood against the wall. Jilly was already there and I sat down beside her. Nobody said anything.

Mom came in and sat on the arm of the sofa. She looked wiped. "The police are going to be here for quite awhile," she told Dad. "They suggested a hotel. Then tomorrow we'll take Lydia down to the station so they can question her again and take her statement."

"I'll call the Quality Inn," Dad said.

"Should I pack a bathing suit?" Jilly nudged me. "They've

got a waterslide."

"This isn't a family vacation!" Mom snapped.

Jilly hung her head. "We're in trouble, aren't we?"

Mom sighed and ran her hand through her hair. "I can't understand why you guys just didn't come to us right away. How many times have we told you, if you're in trouble, come to us, that's what were here for."

I was too tired to defend myself.

"I thought that was just about *drinking*," Jilly mumbled.

Mom threw up her hands in frustration.

"So are we being punished? Are you taking *more* time off my curfew?" Jilly looked like she was about to cry.

"This isn't the time or place. We'll talk about it later," Dad said, and then he turned to me. "Why don't you go have a shower? It'll make you feel better."

The officer heard and came over. "They'll want your clothes. I'll get you an evidence bag."

I glanced down. My arm was covered in dried blood. It was between my fingers and soaked into my watch strap. There was a spray of tiny droplets all over the front of my shirt. My stomach lurched and I thought I might be sick. The bathroom seemed a million miles away. When I got up I felt dizzy.

Jilly must have noticed. She stood up next to me. "Here, lean on me." She held me by the elbow and helped me to my room. "Sit." She pulled out my desk chair. "I'll go turn on the hot water. What do you want to pack for the hotel? I'll throw some stuff in a bag."

"It doesn't matter." I could barely think straight.

"Okay. Don't worry, I'll find something."

"Why are you being so nice to me?"

She didn't answer right away. "I shouldn't have left you alone. I should have made you come with me."

I saw her eyes were watery. "Jilly, there's no way we could have predicted this. That she was this…insane."

"We *should* have predicted it, though. We knew she had a gun."

I shook my head. "No, Jilly. Not us, not *anyone*, could have seen this coming."

She ran her fingers under her eyes. "You should go have your shower," she said in a hoarse voice.

There was a knock. It was the officer. She passed me a large clear bag. "I'll be out here in the hall," she said.

When I came out of the bathroom, Jilly was still in my room, sitting quietly on the end of my bed.

"Here. I got out some comfy clothes for you." She was holding my new T-shirt, the one she'd made me buy, and…her yoga pants? Her prized Lulu Lemons, with the yellow waistband.

"Wow, Jilly, the pants. Thanks."

"No worries," she shrugged. "Listen. I don't think I'm going to be able to sleep much tonight. You?"

I shook my head.

"A movie-athon?"

"Ummm…"

"Don't worry, no horror. I have Vivian's Season One of *The O.C.* We could take it to the hotel."

She was trying so hard. "That'd be great, Jilly."

"I'll wait for you downstairs." On the way to the door she stopped and hugged me.

"Jilly?"

"Yeah?"

"I know I said you couldn't borrow my new shirt. But you can, anytime."

"Oh." She bit her lip and looked down at the floor. "Um, thanks."

After she left, I stood in front of the dresser and stared at myself in the mirror. My hair was wet, my face pale, but other than that, I looked normal. Like nothing had ever happened.

I knew it hadn't sunk in yet, that stuff would hit me later. The fact that things could have ended very differently, that it would be a long time before I'd want to close my eyes again. But for now I just wanted to get through tonight.

I slipped on Jilly's yoga pants and picked up my T-shirt. It wasn't as hideous as I'd remembered. I hadn't even had a chance to wear it yet. It was halfway over my head when I noticed something, or more accurately, smelled something. Strawberries. Jilly's shampoo. I pulled the shirt off and held it up in front of me. There was a lipstick smudge on the neckline and a hole under the arm.

epilogue

(two months later)

It's true what they say about time...that it heals all wounds. Of course some wounds need more than others—like Sam and Megan's. But for me, little by little, things were slowly returning to normal.

It had taken a long time to convince my parents that I was okay. I knew they meant well, but I found it kind of exhausting, the need to constantly reassure them. They couldn't seem to understand that just the fact that Mrs. Swicker was going away for a long time, whether it was prison or some mental institution, was really all I needed to know at that point.

"Don't you want to talk to someone, someone professional?" Mom had asked.

"Like a wrestler?"

Mom hadn't found that funny.

Now that I was back at school, I felt a bit more like myself—must have been the routineness of it all. It was almost a relief, walking out the door in the mornings, knowing I would be just one in a sea of fifteen hundred for the next seven hours.

This morning I lay in bed, face smooshed into my pillow, putting off getting up. My whole Sunday was going to be spent working on a Canadian history assignment. I felt tired just thinking about it.

My stomach grumbled so I headed down to the kitchen.

Jilly was sitting at the table, *trying* to do the crossword from the newspaper. Mom was going through the cupboards jotting down a grocery list.

"Hey," I said.

"Morning," Mom replied.

I opened the fridge and hung off the door, waiting to be inspired by its contents. Anything? Anything? Nothing.

"Lydia. Close the fridge," Mom sighed.

"Sorry." I swung the door closed and leaned my back against the counter. My eyes were immediately drawn to the spot on the floor. I blinked a few times until the image of Mrs. Swicker lying there evaporated. It may have just been my imagination but I could swear I could still see the stains, even after a million cleanings. Everyone had said how good it was that I didn't kill her. I don't think that's how I really feel, but I'll just keep that to myself. Mom would think feelings like that had *therapy* written all over them.

Dragging my eyes from the floor, I turned to the window. Sometimes I worried about these visions that kept flashing through my head, how real they seemed. My entire body would tense up, like I was living the whole thing over again. I told myself it was totally normal. I think I bought it.

I stared at the house across the street, now empty, and thought back to that night, the look on Sam and Megan's faces as they were taken away, the things they said to me.

After some time had passed and things settled down, we eventually got to see them, Sam and Megan. It was just a few weeks ago. The Kennedys invited us to New York for a proper thank you. The entire trip was a whirlwind. Every touristy thing imaginable was scheduled. Sam and Megan the whole time with forced smiles plastered on their faces—there's no way the visit had been their idea. We never got a moment alone to talk about what happened. I think it had been planned that way.

Now we were home and no one talked about it here, either. But that was probably because of me. I certainly wasn't about to strike up any conversations about it.

"Mom, can I use your computer to check my email?" I asked.

"Sure. Just that, though, nothing else."

I ducked into her office and, not bothering to sit down, typed in my password. Impatiently I waited for my inbox to pop up. I had sent three emails to Megan over the last week. She hadn't replied, not once.

"One new message," I whispered. It was from Megan. Slowly I sat down, sort of afraid to click on her name.

Hi Lydia. Sorry I took so long. Wasn't really sure what I wanted to say. It was weird when you came to visit. Did you think that too? Maybe we should have waited longer. When I saw you again, it made me remember everything. I don't think the Kennedys thought about that when they invited you. And I know this is totally chickening out, telling you this in an email instead of to your face, but I was so ashamed of myself. I'm really sorry for all those things I said that night. I know Sam is too. I wanted you to know that, in case you didn't hear from me for a while. Another thing I didn't say to you was "'thank you." Guess I should start a list. :) That's all I got for now. Megan. p.s. I attached the photo Jilly wanted.

I sat quietly for a minute, rereading Megan's words, wondering if I'd ever actually hear from her again. I opened the attached file. It was a picture of Jilly holding a giant cardboard cheque. Reward money from the Kennedys, presented to us when we did an interview on *The Today Show*.

The Today Show…now and forever referred to as "*The Today Show* Fiasco." Even though part of me wanted to forget that whole morning, the other part wished Megan had sent more pictures. I barely remember a thing except for being so nervous I could barely talk. I had to keep clearing my throat over and over again—it must have sounded like I was trying to hack up a hairball. Dad kept checking his armpits for perspiration stains. We actually lost Mom at one point when she found out Sting was the musical guest. And during the interview, Jilly mentioned Vivian's name but practically shouted it into her microphone (Vivian made her promise), which caused wicked feedback and everyone in the studio cringed in pain.

I still feel weird about taking the Kennedys' money. I never expected it, never wanted it, but they insisted. Mom put the money in an account, most of it pegged for university except for an extravagant family vacation we get to plan together, and five hundred dollars to each Jilly and myself to spend on anything we wanted. But not until we'd been subjected to a condensed version of Mom's punishment pyramid. Jilly was down to twenty-four dollars. My money was in an envelope on my desk, under a pile of school binders, still untouched.

Taking another look at Jilly's picture, I had to smile. She seemed to be more fascinated by the giant cheque than the actual money, jumping up and down like she was on a game show or something. I forwarded the photo to her email.

When I went back into the kitchen Jilly was standing by the stove spreading butter on bread. "I'm making grilled cheese. Want one?"

"For breakfast? No thanks."

She shrugged. "Pass me a cheese slice, would ya?"

I took one from the fridge door and tossed it on the counter.

She held it up to the light, turning up her nose. "These are *lights*, I need two."

I rolled my eyes and dug another one out of the package.

"That kind of defeats the purpose, Jilly," Mom said, squirting soap into the sink.

"But Mom, they're *gross*. I don't know why you buy them!"

Mom didn't bother to comment.

"Tommy Cameron's having a party this Saturday, Lid," Jilly said.

Jilly's boyfriend *this* week. "So?"

"Well, do you want to come?"

I looked at her like she was speaking Japanese. "What do you mean do I want to come?"

She sighed. "What do you mean, what do I mean? Do you want to come or not?"

I opened my mouth but didn't know how to answer. I'd never been in this situation before.

Jilly shot me a sly look. "Mitchell Murphy's going to be there and he told me he thinks you're kinda cute."

Mitchell Murphy? He was in grade twelve and...hot. "Can I, Mom?"

I waited for her to answer, but she didn't. Something had caught her attention outside.

"Looks like someone's rented the Henleys' again," Mom

said, leaning slightly towards the window. Jilly and I stopped what we were doing and locked eyes. After a second we tore over to join Mom.

"Please let them have boys," Jilly whispered.

"Please let them *not* be psycho," I whispered.

We stared at the black sedan with a small U-Haul in tow, and held our breath as the car doors swung open.

acknowledgements

Firstly, I would like to thank my family, Ross, Lexi, and William. You never had a doubt. You always believed.

To all my dear friends, old and new, thank you for listening, even when you didn't feel like it. Look close. You'll see glimpses of yourselves in these pages.

And lastly, my writing group. Daph, Jo, Jenn, Cyndy, Joanna, and Graham, saying thank you a million times would never be enough, so one will have to do. "Thank you."